"If you ll
be, I

"I thought you'd been doing that already."

Leanne stopped and faced Mark. Had his voice held a tinge of disappointment? "No, I haven't. I've just been trying to learn everything fast."

She mentally slapped herself. *Don't admit your vulnerabilities.* It gave him an edge, and being so far behind, she couldn't afford to give him any further advantage.

"I'd be happy to help you."

She spun to face him, astounded.

After a moment Mark chuckled. "Well, maybe not happy."

"And maybe not really helpful." She glanced at him. "You don't consider me much of a threat, do you?"

Dear Reader,

Families are funny, you know? What passed for normal in my family of five kids seemed strange to my friend who had only one sibling—and a brother at that. Not to mention what my friend who's an only child thought of our troop! As the youngest, I've always been intrigued by family dynamics, which is why I'm so pleased to have my first book published by Harlequin American Romance, the specialists in stories of home and family. I've dreamed of writing for Harlequin for many years, so this novel is very special to me. My hero and heroine didn't make it easy, however!

The main characters of *Marrying the Boss*, Mark and Leanne, have *very* interesting family backgrounds. I couldn't wait until they showed me how they'd work through their issues and still fall in love. It was a fun ride that I hope you'll enjoy.

I'd love to hear what you think. Please contact me through my Web site, MeganKellyBooks.com.

Sincerely,

Megan Kelly

Marrying the Boss
MEGAN KELLY

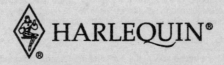

TORONTO • NEW YORK • LONDON
AMSTERDAM • PARIS • SYDNEY • HAMBURG
STOCKHOLM • ATHENS • TOKYO • MILAN • MADRID
PRAGUE • WARSAW • BUDAPEST • AUCKLAND

ISBN-13: 978-0-373-75210-2
ISBN-10:   0-373-75210-5

MARRYING THE BOSS

www.eHarlequin.com

Printed in U.S.A.

ABOUT THE AUTHOR

Fate led Megan Kelly to write romances—fate and her grandmother, that is. While riding a crosstown bus, teenage Megan and her grandma happened on a Harlequin Romance book. The older woman scanned the first page to determine the book's contents and declared it to be about lions, then she gave it to Megan to pass the time on the next day's journey home, five hours away. (The first page did mention lions, but they were statues at the gates of the hero's family estate.) Megan became an avid reader and discovered her dream job—writing those exciting and moving stories she loved. She lives in the Midwest with her husband and two children and is well-known at her local bookstore and library.

For Tom, my real-life Hero—
Thanks for your support on this journey;
and, of course,
For Mom, who taught me by example
about strong women.

Chapter One

Of course the son of a bitch had to be buried in the rain. Leanne Fairbanks glowered at the mausoleum, then yanked her heel out of the mud and advanced toward it.

"Are they all gone, do you think?"

At her mother's question, Leanne surveyed Fields Grove Cemetery—the premiere spot for the dead elite of Chicago. Lionel Collins lay in the family crypt, a large domed building of gray granite, sporting Greek columns and two stone lions for guards. Leanne grimaced at the lions. The egomaniac.

No birds sang. Wet black trees supported branches thinly covered with April buds. Sprinkles of rain made hardly a patter. Dead silence, she thought, then quelled her ill-timed humor. The emptiness of the surroundings unnerved her. "I don't see anyone."

They hadn't attended the private ceremony held in the funeral chapel. Her mom had decided against seeing Gloria, Lionel's daughter-in-law, and her son, Mark, much to Leanne's relief. She'd have gone for support if her mom had felt the need, but personally, Leanne had no use for either of the Collinses. Much as they had no use for her.

They arrived at the mausoleum door, which Leanne was thankful hadn't been locked yet. Two workers turned at their entrance, then ducked out into the drizzle. Their portable floor lamps lit most of the fifteen by fifteen-foot-interior like high noon, illuminating the gaping hole in the wall. Shadows lingered in the corners. Leanne snugged her raincoat tighter.

Her mom closed the umbrella and smoothed her dark-blond hair back into its chignon. At fifty-four, she had only a few lines, although her green eyes had lost their sparkle during the past week.

Giving her mom a moment of privacy, Leanne inspected the crypt. Lionel would be interred above Helen, his wife of forty-seven years. Warren, their son—*my half-brother*—lay at rest across from them. She probed the thought like a sore tooth but experienced no pain. He'd been a stranger, no more than a name to her. Below him was a marker with Gloria's name and birth year chiseled on it.

Leanne frowned. There wasn't a place for Mark.

She started to mention this to her mom, but stopped at the sight of the grief on her face. Her mother's fingertips hovered just above the mahogany casket, tears slipping down her cheeks.

Leanne placed her arm around her mother's shoulders, offering support but no words. She had nothing to say about this man. Other than generous monthly checks, he'd ignored her existence. Conscience money, she thought, then corrected herself. It couldn't have been. Lionel Collins hadn't had a conscience.

Her mother sniffed and dabbed at her tears with a tissue. Leanne hugged her tighter.

"He was a good man. He *was*," her mom emphasized, as though Leanne had argued the point. She wouldn't, not today. If she hadn't changed her mother's mind in the past, debating "the Lion's" questionable merits wouldn't help anything now.

"Yes, he was," a male voice said behind them.

They spun. A tall man filled the doorway, his silky dark hair absorbing the illumination from the workmen's lights. As he stepped forward, she noticed his deep brown eyes and had to repress a shiver. Chilly air, she told herself, wanting to believe it. She recognized him from the financial section of the newspaper.

"I'm sorry," he said. "I thought everyone had headed to the hotel already. My mother lost an earring and is afraid it dropped—" he eyed the casket "—somewhere in here." He leaned forward, hand extended. "I'm Mark Collins."

Leanne gaped when her mother reached to take his hand between both of hers and held on.

"Jenny Fairbanks," she said in her quiet, dignified way. "This is my daughter, Leanne. We're so sorry for your loss."

He placed his other hand over her mother's. He hadn't reacted at all to the introduction. Smooth, Leanne thought.

Mark gestured to the man behind him. "This is Todd Benton. He's come to help me—" again he glanced at the casket "—in my search."

"Leanne Fairbanks?" Todd asked. He stepped forward, his thin eyebrows creeping up on his forehead toward where his hairline should have been. "As well as being a family friend, I'm also the late Mr. Collins's lawyer. I have information of interest to you."

Leanne frowned. "What might that be, Mr. Benton?"

"Your inheritance, of course. I'd like to speak to you in private. Perhaps we could set up a time for you to come to my office."

"What inheritance?" Leanne and Mark said at the same time.

She looked at him, and he glared back. She tried to digest the news while he pierced her with his gaze. His dark eyes narrowed before he turned to the lawyer.

"I seem to be a step behind, Benton. Why is Miss Fairbanks named in my grandfather's will?"

Leanne's mouth dropped open. The nerve of the man. She hadn't expected to inherit anything—nor did she want anything from a man who'd abandoned her mother when she became pregnant. But for Mark to question Lionel's mentioning her was appalling.

"Because she's Lionel's daughter, of course."

"She's *what?*"

He hadn't known? Leanne would have accused him of deception if he hadn't gone pale beneath his tan. Emotions crossed his face, but on such short acquaintance, she couldn't interpret them. He frowned in what could have been confusion. His eyes widened, possibly with disbelief, and was that pain in the tightness around his mouth?

What had the Collins family been told? All these years she thought they'd known about her. If they hadn't, she could forgive their silence. She'd have only Lionel to blame. Perhaps they'd want to embrace her as a member of the family now that they knew.

"His daughter," Benton repeated. "You didn't…? Come on, Mark, you must have known."

Mark shook his head. Had he lost his power of speech? Leanne felt that way herself.

"Gloria and Warren never told you?" Benton asked.

"Mother knows?" Mark whispered, never breaking eye contact with Leanne.

"Of course she knows. Your entire family knew of Lionel's scandal."

A chill washed over Leanne. So much for being embraced.

Benton drew himself upright. "This is obviously not the place for this discussion. Miss Fairbanks, if I may have your current address, I'll contact you with the details of your inheritance."

Leanne broke away from the hold Mark's gaze had on her. She hesitated to leave her mother with Mark, especially after his receiving such news.

After a few hesitant steps, she withdrew a notepad and pen from her purse and jotted down the information. She tore off the paper and handed it to the lawyer. "I wrote my home and work numbers, as well."

"Thank you, Miss Fairbanks. I know this is a hard time for you—"

"Yes," Leanne cut in, then returned to her mother's side. The man had no idea.

"Ms. Fairbanks," Mark said to her, "my mother is waiting at the hotel where we're having the luncheon." He rubbed the back of his neck, then shook his head. "I'm rambling, sorry. I'm still processing this. I want you to come back with me so we can straighten all this out."

Leanne raised an eyebrow. "There's nothing to straighten out. Talking to your mother won't change my paternity. Lionel Collins is—was—my father."

"No one is arguing that point," said Benton. He glanced at Mark. "It would benefit everyone to understand what's at stake here. We could stop at my office."

He turned to her mother and hesitated.

"I don't believe I'll come," her mother said with a slight smile. "I understand Gloria's feelings, and I'm not up to the stares and gossip myself."

"What do you mean 'what's at stake?'" Mark asked.

Benton peered toward the door. The workers stood smoking under the meager shelter of a tree a few feet away.

"I don't give a damn about someone overhearing—"

Benton sighed. "Mark, you don't want it in the news that the Collins heirs were heard fighting at the interment."

"'Heirs?'" Mark voiced Leanne's thought. He looked at her, then her mother.

Leanne put an arm around her mom.

Her mother studied the lawyer. "You said you need to speak with my daughter, Mr. Benton?"

He nodded.

After a moment, she inclined her head, and Benton's shoulders relaxed. What private communication did they just have? Leanne wondered.

Her mother turned to her. "Why don't you go with them, honey? I've got my car. I'm sure they can bring you home after you finish."

"Of course," Mark said. "I'll see to it myself."

Leanne heard his formal tone and took it as reticence. "That won't be necessary. I can afford a cab."

Benton studied his shoes while Mark frowned.

"He's only being polite," her mother said.

Leanne ignored the reprimand. "If we're discussing the will, shouldn't my mother come?"

Mark and Leanne regarded the lawyer, who remained silent. After a moment, Mark looked toward the doorway where rain continued to mist the air.

"Honey." Her mother laid a hand on Leanne's arm. "I don't think I'm mentioned in the will."

Leanne stilled. It wasn't possible. Even Lionel Collins couldn't be that cruel. She awaited the lawyer's denial, but Mr. Benton shook his head. "I'm sorry."

She gazed at her mom's tranquil expression, knowing the hurt it must conceal. Glancing around for someone to contradict this idiocy, she saw Mark looking at her with compassion. No, his concern wasn't aimed at her.

"My grandfather was a hard man," he said to her mother, "as you may know. I'm sorry he's done this to you."

Her mother's lips quavered. "You're a kind man, Mr. Collins."

"No, ma'am, I'm afraid I'm too much like my grand-father."

She cocked her head. "I don't think so. Not in the ways that matter."

Leanne stared at them, disbelieving. What kind of mutual-admiration crap was this? Granted, it wasn't Mark's fault her mother had been slighted, but she'd always thought of the Collinses as the enemy. Now here were her mom and the grandson making eyes at each other.

A kind man, she fumed. As though her mother knew anything about him. And him offering compassion as though he could possibly understand their lives. He'd grown up with his parents and grandparents, attending private schools, with privilege and wealth. Her mother had struggled as a hairdresser, living in a small house in a fading middle-class suburb.

"I'm going home," her mother said. "Call me when you can."

"Mom—"

"Now, dear, you go on. Mr. Benton probably has a lot to explain to you."

Her mother disappeared after shaking hands with the men, while Leanne stood in disbelief. *She's left me to the wolves.*

Mark shook his head. He couldn't imagine even the Lion doing something this heartless. His grandfather's nickname came as much from his way of doing business—territorially, with a snarl and show of fangs for anyone who got too close—as from his given name of Lionel or his mane of blond hair.

Leanne had inherited his hair, along with whatever else he'd left her. Her face had gone white when she'd realized Jenny had been slighted, and her lips had tightened. He had the overwhelming urge to caress her cheek, not only to comfort her, but to enjoy its softness against his fingers.

He cleared his throat, drawing Leanne's attention. Her green eyes appeared darker, with the black center more pronounced than before. Could she be in shock?

She turned to Todd. Her stiff posture and angry expression—not shock, after all—proclaimed her eagerness to get away from them. "Mr. Benton, if you would please send me notice of whatever Lionel felt guilty enough to leave me, I'd appreciate it."

"Well, you see, that may be a problem."

"Why?" she asked.

"The terms of Lionel's will are complicated. It involves two—" He shot a look at Mark. "—uh, inheritances. One is a cash amount. The other is…"

"Spit it out, man." Mark nearly shook the lawyer. He didn't trust that furtive glance Todd had given him. Something was up.

"We should really discuss this in my office," Benton said. "Perhaps we could just ride over there—"

"I need to get back to the luncheon," Mark said.

"And I have no intention of going anywhere with you two."

This startled Mark, as well as Benton, judging by the open mouth of the other man.

"I don't intend to be rude," Leanne said a little more quietly, "but I also need to go comfort my mother." She glared at Mark.

He hadn't meant to be insensitive. He wasn't even sure how he'd managed to ruffle her feathers, but she was incensed. Her first statement about not going anywhere with them rang truer than this half excuse of comforting her mother—even though the poor woman did need consoling, Mark thought.

"Just give her the highlights," Mark said.

Benton sighed, then nodded. "I suppose as you're the principles involved, I could do that here. I want you to know I did try to dissuade him, Mark." He cleared his throat. "Lionel has set you up in competition against each other."

Mark looked at Leanne. Her furrowed brow told him she shared his confusion. "What competition?"

"There are three tasks you must complete. Whichever of you completes two tasks first, to the satisfaction of the board of directors, wins."

Mark drew a breath. He had a long association with the Lion's manipulation tactics. This wouldn't be good. "Just what do we win?"

Benton straightened. "The winner gets all of Lionel's stock in the Collins Company and thereby his position as CEO."

Mark clenched his jaw. "That bastard."

"Do you mind?" Leanne said. "I really dislike that term."

He blinked, reminded of her presence. When he caught her meaning, he said, "Sorry. I meant, that son of a bitch."

She inclined her head. "Thank you."

He couldn't look away from her. His competition. For CEO. Dear God, he couldn't believe it. He'd been training for that position since his father had died ten years before, training with the Lion himself. Now it could all be snatched away from him at the whim of a controlling old bas—son of a bitch.

For years, he'd tried to prove himself worthy of the Collins name. He'd thought his position as successor secure, as he was the only Collins left, other than his mother.

Until Leanne Fairbanks appeared, Lionel's blood relative. Blood had mattered to Lionel, which was why Mark had tried so hard to make the old man forget his adoption. He'd modeled himself after his father and Lionel. Working all hours, he'd not only burned the midnight oil, but often the 3:00 a.m. oil as well. No matter what successes he achieved, he knew the Lion regarded him as not-quite-a-Collins. He swallowed back his sense of betrayal.

"I don't suppose there's been some mistake," Mark said without much hope.

"No," Benton said. "Lionel stated very clearly his intentions—"

Leanne opened her mouth, but before a sound could emerge, Mark cut in. "There must be a loophole."

"The will is airtight, I assure you," Benton replied.

Leanne made a sound, but Mark turned his back on her. *Think.* There had to be a solution. This was nuts.

He snapped his fingers and turned back to Benton.

"I'll contest it," he said. "I'll declare the old Lion non compos mentis. It's insane, giving the business to an outsider. The place will be run into the ground inside a week. No judge in the world would consider this the design of a rational man."

"Your grandfather was in no way impaired when he devised the will," Benton said. "I tried to talk him out of it, Mark, but it was his money, his company and his prerogative on how to dispose of it."

"*Dispose of it* is right. He might as well have sold the place for scrap as to hand it over to…" His voice trailed off, and he turned to face Leanne.

"Yes?" She smiled. "You were saying?"

He ducked his head for a moment, then met her gaze. "I apologize, Ms. Fairbanks. I was on the verge of being impolite, but I'm sure you agree how crazy the idea is."

"Do I?"

Mark stared at her. She blinked down at her hands,

which she'd gripped together. When she raised her head again, he couldn't read her expression.

He found his voice. "I shouldn't have to buy the company I've worked for my whole life. It should be mine."

"Why?" Leanne asked.

"Because— Did you ask why? You, who I didn't even know existed until twenty minutes ago?"

She raised her chin. "Yes."

"Well, then, I'll tell you, Ms. Fairbanks. I've lived with the company since I was a baby. I learned the inner workings of every aspect of each department. I sat at the dinner table with the Lion, celebrated holidays with him, worked at his side. I'm the heir apparent."

Leanne smirked. "Apparently not."

Mark's jaw tightened. He'd walked right into that one, but couldn't retract his words. The *heir apparent*, for God's sakes. He didn't talk like that. No one talked like that.

He swallowed down his embarrassment and reined in his anger. It wasn't her fault the Lion had betrayed him.

Dammit. The company should be his, without any question. Without any qualification or restriction. Without any idiotic contest.

"Oh, my God," he groaned. "It's that TV show."

Benton nodded. "Your grandfather always admired the Donald. He drew up this will after the show first aired. I advised against it."

Mark ran a hand over his face. He couldn't believe he'd have to earn his place all over again.

Leanne cleared her throat.

Mark narrowed his eyes at her. A pink tinge from the cool April air nearly covered the pale freckles on her cheeks. He couldn't be distracted by her. She embodied his new competition. *No, don't think about her body.* Still, he gave her slender form a once-over, noting the snug waist below nicely rounded breasts.

"If I'm following you," Leanne said, cutting short his inspection, "Lionel's will is based on a reality TV show?"

Benton nodded. "*The Apprentice*. Young business people compete to win a job with Donald Trump."

"Then," Mark interrupted, "we can definitely declare the Lion out of his mind."

"He was mentally competent," Benton stated again.

"Nevertheless, I plan to contest the will. The Collins Company will not go to a stranger." He paused, feeling a moment's regret for Leanne's feelings, but determined all the same. "I won't lose control of the company to anyone, family or not."

"IT WAS dreadful," Leanne told her mom later in her mother's living room, having taken a cab rather than accept a ride from Mark Collins. She swirled her lemonade. She'd angled herself on the couch facing her mother, who was wedged against the opposite corner. They'd sat like this for years, whether to gossip or have a heartfelt conversation. "He was so angry, so hurt. He wouldn't let me say anything. I meant to say I didn't want the damned company, that I didn't want anything from Lionel." Nothing for myself, she thought. Recognition of her mother's loyalty and some money so her mother could retire would have been nice.

Leanne sighed. She didn't want the company, but she wouldn't be dismissed as worthless. She'd been overlooked and neglected by the Collins family her entire life. To have her ability to run the company compared to scrapping the place had irritated her.

"Oh, dear," her mom said when she didn't continue. "What did you do?"

Leanne shook her head, feeling idiotic. "Exactly what you're afraid of, I'm sure. I let my feelings run away with me. My mouth ran with them, charging ahead without my permission."

Her mom laughed. "You're too blond to have such a temper. If you'd let me dye your hair red, people would at least have a warning." She patted Leanne's hand. "So, are you going to compete for the company with the boy?"

"'The boy' is four years older than I am, as you well know." Lionel had admitted to her mother he had a family, Leanne would give him that. He'd been honest, in his way.

"Will you do it?" her mom asked.

Leanne didn't know. Her pride had taken a hit with Mark's vehement rejection. By naming her in the will, Lionel had acknowledged her as his daughter. To inherit some money mollified her pride. To be given a chance to take over CoCo, as she and her mother referred to the Collins Company, confused her.

She'd wanted Lionel to honor her mother with an inheritance as well, no matter how small the amount.

"I'm not sure," she said when she realized her mother still awaited her answer.

"Could you?"

"What? Take it from him?" At her mother's nod, she

shrugged. "I could give him a run for his money, I think. But what would I do if I won?"

"Control CoCo."

"I'm pretty happy teaching at the university, Mom. What would I want with their company?"

Her mother's gaze dropped to her own glass. "Revenge?"

Leanne stilled. Avenge her mother? She swallowed. "But…I thought you loved Lionel and didn't regret your time together?"

Her mother nodded but didn't raise her head.

"Mom." She laid her hand over her mother's.

Her mother looked at her, her eyes wet with unshed tears. "I gave him up and never saw him again. I was the other woman, Lee. I knew I wouldn't get to keep him. I never intended to take him away from his family. I just wanted him, for however long he could stay."

Leanne didn't understand that kind of thinking. If she loved someone, she'd want him all to herself.

Her mother sniffed and sipped from her lemonade glass. "Did you like the boy?"

"Please stop calling him that. His name is Mark."

Her mother winced, and Leanne cursed her clumsy tongue. Mark had been Lionel's middle name.

"Although from the way he acted," Leanne teased, "you'd think it was Barnabus Collins."

Her mother laughed, as Leanne had hoped, picking up her reference to an old TV show about vampires. "I'm sure that was just the eerie setting. I didn't notice any pointy teeth, but he definitely had hypnotic eyes."

"Full of deep-brown sin," Leanne agreed.

"Better and better," her mother said, wiggling her eyebrows. "He's certainly handsome enough to be supernatural."

"Yeah." Leanne sighed. "More's the pity."

"Why?"

"Mother, he's not only the enemy, he's my nephew."

Chapter Two

Mark poured himself a drink, downed it, then poured another. It had been that kind of day. The alcohol burned his throat, and he tried not to wince at the bitterness. He never could stand the taste. Another reason Father and the Lion thought he was too soft.

"I'll take one of those," his mother said, entering the sitting room.

"Don't you want to ask what I'm having?"

"It doesn't matter. After your news, I'll drink anything."

He poured his mother a Scotch on the rocks and took it to where she lay on the couch. Except for her sharp dark-blue eyes, she looked weary, her face wilted. She'd swung her feet onto the couch, black spiked heels and all, and reclined as though the effort to sit upright was beyond her. Not a hair escaped her expensively maintained blond twist.

Taking a seat in the Queen Anne chair across from her, he reviewed what he wanted to ask. He'd have to proceed carefully. If his mother didn't like his tone, he'd never find out anything.

"What can you tell me about Leanne Fairbanks?"

Gloria opened an eye for a moment, then put the cold glass back against her forehead. "She's the Lion's daughter."

"She's about my age."

"Hmm? Oh, she's thirty."

"I was four. So, Grandmother was alive." He hated to state the obvious, but he needed to gently lead his mother into disclosing pertinent details. If he didn't finesse his way around her, she'd close up. "Did she know?"

His mother snorted. "Your grandmother knew everything, from the moment he first saw the tramp. Helen knew every time they got together, God help her."

"I don't understand. Grandmother would never have put up with the Lion having an affair."

"You think not? This wasn't his first, although it was his last. I'm sure this girl is the only illegitimate child we'll have to deal with. The Lion was careful. The tramp must have tricked him."

Mark clenched his teeth. He couldn't refer to Jenny as "the tramp," but he didn't want to dissuade his mother from talking, no matter what terms she used. He could only be thankful she'd called Leanne illegitimate, not something worse.

"So," he said, "this woman had an affair with the Lion and got pregnant. Then what?"

She shrugged. "Then nothing. Helen insisted he 'come home and stop this silliness,' I believe were her words."

"And he did." It wasn't a question. Mark knew the Lion. If Grandmother said come home, then home he'd come. "Are you sure he had multiple affairs?"

Gloria drained her glass. "You *are* naive."

"He seemed very much in love with Grandmother."

She laughed, the sound grating on Mark's nerves. He put up with it because she was his mother and she'd had a trying day, but he didn't have to like it. As soon as he got his facts, he'd head for his own condo in the city.

"Mark, you're either going to kill me or keep me young. I just don't know where you get that sentimental streak. Yes, yes." She rose and went to the drinks cart. "He loved Helen. He adored her, but he cheated on her. I believe it was about power and an illusion of youth. I've never understood how she could turn the other cheek, which she did until the tramp got pregnant. That she couldn't abide." His mother glowered into her glass. "We thought she'd gotten rid of the kid. Obviously, we were wrong."

Mark snapped his mouth closed. Who was this person speaking so casually of "getting rid of the kid," as though the baby weren't important, as though it weren't family? Not the mother who'd adopted him to fill a yearning for a child she couldn't conceive. Not the mother he'd known all these years.

Of course, he thought he'd known the Lion. He'd never have believed the Lion would cheat on his wife. Nor that Grandmother would accept it, as long as no children came from such a union. So maybe he didn't know his mother. Or his father, either.

"Did Father ever…step out?"

Gloria chuckled. "Darling," she said, dropping ice cubes as punctuation, "I am not—*click*—the type to turn the other cheek. *Click* Your father never strayed. *Click, click.*

Mark let go the breath he'd been holding. His world had

changed that afternoon, but some truths still held. "Did the Lion know Leanne hadn't been…? Of course, he must have known she existed to have named her in the will."

"I've been thinking about that." His mother fell back on the couch, not spilling a drop.

Practice? Mark reproached himself for the thought. The revelations of the day had his head spinning.

"I think," she continued, "the Lion must have kept in touch. Not while Helen lived. He'd never dishonor her wishes that way."

But he'd sleep around on her? Mark began to feel as though he'd grown up in a madhouse.

"Perhaps he got in contact after Helen died," Gloria said. "What matters is that Leanne's here."

"We'll talk to the company's lawyer. If we can't have the will overturned due to its unusual nature—which reflects on the Lion's mental stability at the time of writing it—"

"Benton will testify Lionel had full possession of his faculties."

Gloria waved a hand in dismissal. "Of course he will. He'll be protecting his hide. Our lawyer will make sure the judge understands that."

Mark could only marvel at his mother's keen mind. Devious and a little scary, but since she acted from love for him, he couldn't complain. "And if that doesn't work?"

"We'll buy her off."

"No, Mother, we won't."

"I'll get millions from the Lion."

"Whatever money you get should be yours."

Gloria leaned forward and grasped his hand, her scarlet

nails biting. "What better thing to spend it on? You deserve control of the company, Mark. The Lion had to have been crazy even to think of handing it over to anyone else."

"She's not just anyone. She's his daughter. His blood."

"Is that what's bothering you?" She leaned back. "The Lion loved you, Mark, as much as he loved his own son."

He nodded, telling himself it might be true.

"In the meantime," his mother said, "I'll get our lawyer to recommend a private detective for the case. See what we can find out about little Miss Fairbanks. And her mother."

Mark opened his mouth, then closed it and looked away. It didn't sit right, but he knew it to be a wise course of action. *Know thy enemy.*

Especially if the enemy possessed killer legs.

LEANNE READ her letter to her mother. "'You are to convene at the Collins Company boardroom next Tuesday or forfeit your chance to be named Chief Executive Officer.'"

She'd scanned it herself, then brought the notice to her mother's house to discuss. "I don't want to go."

"What do you mean?" her mom demanded. "Gloria and the boy stood in front of a judge and tried to have your father declared insane. If you don't show up, it's like saying you agree."

Three weeks had passed since the revelations in the mausoleum. Her letter had arrived by registered mail, relating the details in "lawyer language" and citing the amount of her cash inheritance. A very nice nest egg. Her mother could retire, and Leanne could quit teaching if she wanted.

Mr. Benton had told Leanne the Collins Company lawyer had argued with Gloria against bringing the case to court on the grounds it would hurt the company's image. Gloria pursued it nevertheless. A judge, who, according to Gloria, "didn't have the sense God gave tree sap," had pronounced the will valid. She had turned the air blue when they lost.

Leanne paced the living room. "Why would I want to run CoCo? I'm not even sure I could, but I don't want it. I don't want anything from that family. They've had no use for me for the past thirty years. I have no use for them now."

Her mother stepped in front of her, bringing Leanne to a halt. "Sit. You're making me dizzy." She dragged her onto the sofa beside her. "Now, listen. Your father pro—"

"Please don't call him that. He doesn't deserve—"

"Your father," she insisted, "provided for you. I received a check every month after he left, before you were even born. I got a check in my eighth month to cover all my doctor and hospital fees."

"As if he's some hero for doling out money. Mom, he was rich—filthy, disgustingly rich. It was a payoff so you wouldn't make trouble."

"Lionel knew I wouldn't make trouble. He gave me money to provide for us. For your safe delivery and care. Every month," she stressed, "a nice check came in the mail."

"I know, Mom. I get it. Conscience money."

"He loved me, Lee."

Leanne bit her lip and dropped her gaze to their clasped hands. If her mother needed to believe that, she wouldn't argue.

"And he cared about you. That's what the money meant. That's why he mentioned you in the will."

"But not you."

The silence hung between them. Leanne wanted to cry out, *If he loved you so much, where's your inheritance?* But she wouldn't hurt her mother with bitter words.

"Let it go, honey," her mom said quietly. "I've had thirty years with you. That's gift enough."

Leanne laid her head on her mother's lap, fighting back tears. "You're unbelievable."

She stroked a hand through Leanne's hair. "I loved him. When you love someone, that's all that matters. I didn't care that he was rich. Or married."

Leanne sat up. "That's so unlike you."

"I hope you find a love like that, Leanne."

She grinned. "You want me to have an affair with a rich married man?"

Her mom chucked her playfully on the chin. "Smarty-pants. I want you to experience a love that will take your breath away. That makes you reexamine everything you thought you knew about yourself. That makes you a new person."

"I don't want to have to change to keep some guy. That's not who I am."

Her mom frowned. "Is that what you think of me?"

"I don't know. You never imagined you'd ever be with a married man. Then Lionel Collins came along and you changed."

"He swept me away. I can't explain it any better. I saw things in him no one else saw, not even his wife. He was gentle and fun and amazing in bed."

"Eeew! Don't tell me stuff like that. You're my mother."

Her mom leaned toward her and whispered, "I've had sex."

"Stop it." Leanne laughed and made her index fingers into a cross to ward her off. "Besides, this is about me taking over CoCo."

"Well, for one thing, we'll have to stop calling it CoCo. Keep in mind, whoever runs Collins inherits Lionel's stock and gets control of the company."

"Yeah, Mr. Benton explained that." Leanne picked at the seam of a pillow. "Mark looked so hurt by it all."

"By what?"

"Lionel's putting him up against me for CoCo."

"That's business."

"He took it personally. I feel bad. It's wrong, somehow, to fight him for this."

Her mom's hand rested on hers. "If you don't want to do it, just tell them."

"It's just more trouble. I'm not part of the family."

"So, you don't want your inheritance, either?"

Leanne heard the hurt in her mother's voice. By not taking these gifts—if the challenge for CoCo could be called a gift—she rejected Lionel, as well. "Oh, no, I'm accepting the money. There's enough for you to buy a nice home in New Mexico or Arizona. You can retire from cutting hair and being on your feet all day."

"No, the money is for you. Buy something you'll enjoy."

Leanne smiled. "You think I won't enjoy visiting you someplace nice and warm in the middle of winter? Or sitting by your pool in the summer?"

"Oh, I'm getting a pool now, huh? Well, okay." She sighed, a smile dancing in her eyes. "If it'll make you happy."

MARK PACED the conference room, glancing at the clock. "Mother, it's time. I'm going in there alone." He held up his palm to halt her interruption. "I'll give you all the details on what transpires."

"I should go with you. I'll buy the girl out. Teachers don't get paid that much. She'll know she can't compete against you. It's a smart move."

He rubbed the back of his neck. Their personal lawyer had obtained information on Leanne. She held a Master's degree in Business Management and taught at the University of Illinois at Chicago. "She might not have any appreciable business experience, Mother, but she's not stupid."

He picked up the investigator's report from their lawyer. "She's not just a teacher, she's a professor. Well-respected."

"But not tenured."

"She's young for that."

"Mark, the girl is no competition."

"I agree. I just don't want to see her embarrassed. She *is* family." And that, he told himself, was the only reason he cared.

"Oh, please."

"Even with the agreements, it'll be difficult to keep this fiasco out of the papers. Too many people know already. The court case didn't help. If I have to wipe the floor with my young auntie, I will. I'd just rather not endure a public farce while doing it."

"She's hardly worth your concern."

"I'm concerned with keeping the business. I'm going to run it, as we've always planned."

"Maybe you should charm the girl, keep her off balance. Just don't let this little Miss-Nothing-from-Nowhere bring down the business with a scandal. No one needs to hear about her harlot mother becoming the Lion's mistress or raising his illicit offspring all on her own."

Mark swung around to berate his mother, but stopped. Leanne stood in the doorway, ashen and wide-eyed. He took a step toward her.

Leanne backed away. Her gaze held his, and it seemed she checked her tears by sheer force of will.

"So you're here," Gloria said. "I suppose it's time for you two to get your first assignment."

Leanne nodded slowly, then straightened her shoulders. "Yes, I do believe it's time to begin."

Mark followed her out the door to the next room, unsure what to say. He could strangle his mother for her hateful words. He wished he'd had the chance to defend Leanne. He felt awful. The poor woman had stepped into a vicious world of cutthroat dealings. She'd be out of her element. No one was exempt from cruelty here. No matter how stunning her green eyes, how shapely her legs.

He pulled his thoughts back into line. This woman, for all her claim to be related to his adopted father, was a stranger. A stranger who would try to take his birthright from him.

Well, no, he checked himself. Actually, it was her birthright. His by right of adoption and years of damned hard work. He was the non-blood Collins, the outsider. They were related only on paper.

Does that mean we could...?

With an irritated grunt, he stepped into the room behind her. Introductions had taken place while he'd been standing in the hall like an idiot.

"Mr. Mulvany." Mark reached across and shook the man's hand. He greeted each of the six board members and Todd Benton. He watched Leanne slide into a chair, then took the one next to her. They sat facing the board across the table. He shook his head. *Just like on the TV show.*

Harrison Mulvany III reached inside his coat pocket and slid a white envelope across the table to Leanne. "I've been entrusted with this, my dear. I don't know the contents myself. I'm just passing along a favor."

He reached into his pocket, then slid a cream envelope toward Mark. Mark watched out of the corner of his eye as Leanne slit hers open. Her mouth tightened; her eyes narrowed.

He slit open his own envelope. The Lion had left him a brief note: "I'm counting on you to prove I haven't wasted all these years. Prove you're a Collins."

Mark very carefully folded the note, then fitted it back into the envelope. He put it in his inside breast pocket, against his heart.

When would he fit in? What the hell did he have to do to finally belong to this family?

The Lion had just answered those questions. He'd fit in when he won. Only then would he prove he was a Collins.

"No," Leanne said.

He looked at her, forgetting she'd just received a note from the dead, also.

"I'm not interested."

Mulvany nodded, then slid her a cream-colored envelope. "From your father."

Mark started. This one came from the Lion? "May I ask who the first note was from?"

She turned her head and looked right through him. "I'm sure you know." Then she turned her attention to the sheet of stationery. After a moment, she put it in her purse.

Benton cleared his throat. "Shall we begin?"

Mulvany nodded.

"You've met the board members," Benton said. "They wanted an opportunity to look you over. Now all but Mr. Mulvany, Mr. Garland and Mrs. Metcalf will leave."

The other four filed out. The door closed, and silence descended. Mark's throat tightened. He knew he would win. Leanne had no experience while he'd had twenty years working right here at Collins Company. Still, the tension of being measured against the Lion's expectations bored into his head.

Benton opened a folder in front of him. "This is how we proceed. I have given the first challenge to Mr. Mulvany, who will oversee the competition. The three board members present will reconvene after each challenge's time limit to review your effort. They will determine who wins each phase. The last challenge carries the most weight in their determination of the winner for the position of CEO and control of the Lion's stock shares. Questions?"

Leanne shook her head.

Mark asked, "Is there any recourse other than this competition?"

"I'm sorry, but no," Benton said. "Should either of you

choose not to compete, you will be disqualified. The CEO position and stocks will be awarded to the other person."

Mark looked at the board members. "As acting head—" It grated on him to phrase it that way. He should be in charge. "—of Collins, I want a written promise from each of you to ensure total confidentiality. This would hurt the company should it turn up in the papers."

He withdrew affidavits for each member and slid them across the table. "The Collins lawyers drew these up. You may have your lawyers look at them, but know that I will not continue with any discussion of this farce until these are signed."

Taking the last paper out of the folder, he set it in front of Leanne.

She looked at it, then him. With raised eyebrows, she asked, "Where's yours?"

"My what?"

"I want a guarantee of your silence, as well."

"Trust me, I don't want this to get out."

"Nor do I. However, in the interest of fair play—" Her cold glare indicated that she considered him incapable of being fair. His neck warmed, but he held her gaze when it clashed with his.

"I want to make sure," she continued, "that when the challenges are awarded in my favor, and should I be granted succession of the line—"

Her cat-like smirk reminded him of his "heir apparent" remark in the mausoleum. Heat crept from his neck to his cheeks, and he only hoped it didn't show on his face. He allowed a smile to flirt with his lips, acknowledging her jab, but not bowing before it.

Her smile flashed, then disappeared. "I want to be assured you won't run to the papers to cry foul or try to destroy CoCo once you no longer head it."

"CoCo?"

Her cheeks appeared a shade pinker. "Our pet name for the Collins Company."

"'*Our* pet name?' Yours and your mother's?"

At the mention of her mother, Leanne's face hardened. A sore spot. Good to know, although he doubted he'd use it against her in business. However, the knowledge might come in handy for their private jousts.

Leanne turned back to the table. "Mr. Benton, do you see anything in this document that would make you advise a client against signing?"

"No, it looks standard. However, I would advise you to seek your own counsel—"

"Very well," Leanne cut in. "Thank you. Now, if we could make a copy of this please? I wouldn't want Mr. Collins to be without his own copy to sign."

She sat back and crossed her arms.

Mark nodded to Benton, who rose and called in the Lion's secretary, Mrs. Pickett. While Benton handed her the paper and gave her instructions in a low voice, Leanne sat up and spoke to the board.

"I notice you obey the directives of Mr. Collins. He has merely to nod, and his wishes are fulfilled. I would hope that as we are competing for the same prize and I might be appointed the head of this company, you will award me the same honor."

The board members shifted in their seats.

"What are you saying, Ms. Fairbanks?" Mark asked.

"If this is to be a fair game, so to speak, I will need the aid of the staff as well. I know you've worked for the loyalty you command. I don't expect any. I'm sure I'm considered an interloper. Little Miss Nobody from Nowhere."

Her arrow hit its target. Mark couldn't let that pass without comment. "I'm sorry you overheard that, Leanne," he said quietly. "My mother is very upset."

She threw him a look that expressed her disinterest in his mother's feelings.

"Please understand that her opinions are not necessarily mine," he said.

"But then, to you, I'm just the 'auntie' you're going to wipe the floor with."

He turned away. He wouldn't apologize for his determination to win control of the Collins Company or to prove himself worthy.

"Ms. Fairbanks," Mr. Mulvany said, "I will oversee this farce, as Mark calls it. Rest assured you'll be given every cooperation. I've been informed you're the Lion's natural child. Lionel Collins held my respect as a businessman and a friend. May I say welcome to you, and good luck."

She tipped her head in acknowledgment. With queenly presence, Mark thought.

"Thank you," she said. "Under those conditions and with your conscientious administration of the contest, I will agree to compete."

Mulvany beamed.

Mark swore under his breath. With one show of vulnerability, Leanne had made Mulvany her champion. From the smiles on the faces of the other two board members, Mark knew favor had shifted to her. Now he was the big baddie, trying to trick this sweet young innocent out of her inheritance.

He set his shoulders. Fine. She'd won this round by getting them on her side. Mulvany would look out for her welfare. It wouldn't be easy for him to overcome her personal victory, but he would. Just because they liked her didn't make her a good businesswoman.

Mrs. Pickett returned with the papers, which he and Leanne both signed. Benton took possession of all the documents. "I'll have copies made for your attorney."

"Thank you," she said. "I have no qualms about proceeding."

"Then, here it is," Mr. Mulvany said. "The first challenge is for each of you to make a proposal of something Collins Company—CoCo, if I may?" He smiled at Leanne, who nodded.

Mark simmered.

"Something CoCo needs," he continued. "Whether this be a new product, a new client to sign, a company to take over, or something else will be up to you. I'm sorry to say this, Ms. Fairbanks, as it seems unfair to rush you, but the time limit is two weeks. We are to reconvene in this room to hear your proposals."

Mark gritted his teeth. The man favored her, but did he have to fawn like that?

"At that time," Mulvany continued, "we three will decide which of you developed the better proposal. We will then move on to phase two of the challenge."

"I'm eager to begin," Leanne said, her gaze fixed on Mark.

He admired her boldness and her courage. The challenge in her eyes had blood rushing to his groin. "I can hardly wait."

Chapter Three

Leanne swallowed a sigh as she inspected the Collins financial reports. CoCo basically owned every kind of small firm imaginable. Everything one needed, CoCo had taken over a company that made it. They specialized in buying small- to medium-sized companies, revamping them with either an administrative clean sweep or a production overhaul, then selling the company again for a profit.

She would lose this challenge to Mark, and her lack of knowledge irked her. She didn't know of any business in trouble. She couldn't find any product CoCo needed to make at the companies it currently owned. Leanne tossed the report on her desk to rub her temples. Mark had found her a middle-management-sized office. She'd had no inclination, nor time, to decorate it, so it sat bare and uninspiring with its beige walls and carpet. It felt unused, unmoved-into, just a transitory space.

Leanne sighed. Pretty soon, she wouldn't even have a temporary spot at Collins. She'd be back at school in her real office. Fortunately, she'd been scheduled to teach one night class on Monday and two day classes which met

Tuesdays and Thursdays. She'd shown up at CoCo Monday, Wednesday and Friday of the last two weeks, sometimes in a catatonic state, but trying nevertheless. For all the good it would do her.

Mark, however, didn't share that problem. He knew which companies CoCo had been looking at for takeover. He'd come up with ideas for products to manufacture. Glancing at her desk made her groan; she owned several Collins desk accessories, although, since they sported the brand name, Mark of Excellence, she hadn't known that. All the Mark of Excellence products had begun as Mark Collins's ideas. His little improvements on everyday items had made CoCo a fortune.

An idea for a new product line stumped her. She'd looked into their client list and drawn a blank there, too. She hated to admit defeat, but the challenge ended tomorrow.

"Something I can help you with?"

Leanne stiffened at the sound of Mark's voice at her doorway. She gave him a small, tight smile. "No, I'm fine."

They'd run into each other as she'd inspected different departments in the company. He exuded confidence and control. Mark ran the operations as acting head until the competition decided their futures. Never had she seen him so much as ruffle his hair in frustration over the double stresses of keeping CoCo going and vying for the right to do so.

"Have you had lunch?"

She eyed him. Every time she saw him, he wore a dark business suit. This one, a navy blue, showed off his wide shoulders, narrow waist and long legs. Mark always appeared professionally turned out. His hair lay in tidy near-black neatness. His tie always coordinated.

She felt underdressed. Her brown pantsuit had worked at the university but didn't fit here. No doubt she looked harassed and wrinkled compared to his cool assurance. She'd never be able to think of an answer to the challenge. She had so much to learn—

"Leanne?"

Pulled from her panic over the project, Leanne couldn't remember his question. "I'm sorry. What did you say?"

"Have you had lunch?"

His faint smile annoyed her. He knew all too well she hadn't been eating at the lunchroom here. He knew she hadn't come up with a product or a client or—

"Is that a no?"

She shook her head. "No." *No, I haven't eaten, and no, I won't eat with you.*

"Well, if you have time, I'd like to take you to lunch."

She opened her mouth to decline. He raised his palm to halt her.

"Before you say no, let me suggest a truce. No company talk. I thought maybe we should get to know one another." His shoulders moved in an awkward shrug. "We are family, of a sort."

His suggestion threw her off-balance. Although formal, it was still an overture. She didn't expect him to be charming or personable, but here he was, reaching out to her. She could ignore the rush of attraction she felt, but she couldn't deny its existence. Mark usually came across as aloof, except in Gloria's presence. Then he seemed rigid and proper, with a fine edge of tension.

Gloria. Something niggled at the back of Leanne's mind. Something to do with this lunch invitation and his mother, but she couldn't recall it. Without a valid reason to excuse herself, Leanne said, "Lunch would be nice."

Mark grinned, and she had to catch her breath. Genuine humor lit his eyes, created dimples and nearly made her swoon. If he weren't off-limits to her, she might have had to reach for support. She'd never seen this side of him.

"That's a very cautious acceptance," he said, "but since you did agree, I'm holding you to it. Maybe after we've had lunch, you'll find out I'm not so bad. Next time I ask, you might even say, 'yes, thank you, I'd be delighted.'"

Leanne laughed, rising. "One can hope."

He crooked his arm to escort her. She stared. Was he kidding? Besides being ridiculously old-fashioned, she would appear to be flirting with him. The Collins people would never take her seriously. "Shall I get my coat or are we eating in?"

"Let's not eat here. We'd never have a quiet moment, and all eyes would be on us."

She murmured her agreement as she reached his side. Whenever they'd been in the same room, all activity had stopped while the employees observed them. It unnerved her, which she tried to hide. She had enough pressure to deal with at CoCo; she didn't need constant scrutiny. "If you'd just let me know where you'll be, I could try to avoid you."

"I thought you'd been doing that already."

Leanne stopped. Had his voice held a tinge of disappointment? "No, I haven't. I've just been running around the place, trying to learn everything fast."

She mentally slapped herself. *Don't admit your vulnerabilities.* It gave him an edge, and being so far behind in matters of the company, she couldn't afford to give him any further advantage.

"I'd be happy to help you."

She spun to face him, astounded.

His mouth hung open, his brown eyes wide. He looked so stunned, Leanne laughed. After a moment, Mark chuckled. "Well," he said, "maybe not happy."

"And maybe not really helpful."

He shook his head, still smiling. "I'd like to assure you of my willingness and honorable intentions, but I'm just not that good a person."

"You're human." She grabbed her jacket and purse. "In the same situation, I wouldn't help you, either."

He stared at her. She flashed a grin as she walked past him. His quiet laughter reached her. Maybe lunch with Mark wouldn't be so bad, after all.

He hailed a taxi at the curb. "Moving my car just isn't worth the hassle. I hope you don't mind?"

She shook her head, well-acquainted with Chicago parking.

They got out at a Chinese restaurant near enough to CoCo that they could have walked. Maybe multimillionaires didn't walk, she mused. Glancing around the room, Leanne didn't recognize anyone. They chose a table against an inner wall for privacy. A fish tank sat in the middle of the dark paneling. "Not the CoCo—I mean, the Collins Company executives' favorite lunch spot?"

Mark smiled. "Which is why I chose it."

"Don't want to be seen fraternizing with the enemy?"

"There's that, and I thought it would be more private. I'd like to get to know you, since you're the Lion's daughter."

Leanne narrowed her eyes, pretending to study the menu as the waitress set their tea before them. She doubted his motives and for good reason. "You've had thirty years to get to know me, Mark. I may be just a business professor, but don't play me for a fool."

"You think I have some other reason?"

She glanced at him. His raised eyebrow gave him a pompous, cynical air. His arrogance stiffened the hairs on her neck. "You don't consider me much of a threat, do you?"

His gaze dropped to the menu.

Perhaps it was better he didn't answer, she thought. Then she wouldn't have to dump that tiny cup of weak, lukewarm tea in his lap and walk out. With a small smile, she pictured him blotting tea off his crisp slacks.

They ordered crab Rangoon and egg drop soup to start.

"Everything on the menu looks good," Leanne said to break the silence. "I'm not picky if I don't have to cook." She calculated how much time she could afford to take for lunch. She needed to do some grading. She usually ate at her desk, reading, grading and adjusting her lesson plans. Although it would have been wise to chat up some of CoCo's administration during lunch, she had two demanding "jobs" and couldn't take the time. She had to preserve the job that paid. "Maybe the Hunan chicken."

"Then I'll get the Mongolian beef. We can share."

The simple suggestion shouldn't have bothered her, but the idea of sharing anything with Mark made her frown. The waitress appeared and took their orders.

"You want just plates?" the waitress asked. "Or I bring it family-style? You serve selves. Take what want."

Mark frowned. "We'll have it... We'll serve ourselves."

The little woman jerked her head up and down several times and left.

He couldn't even say "family-style." Leanne swallowed. What a disaster. She couldn't be a casual friend with this man. He represented all the pain from her childhood, and he obviously had issues of his own regarding her.

"So," Mark said, "how's it going at Collins?"

She shrugged.

"I'm not trying to find out what you're doing." He glanced at the fish tank, drawing her eye to it also. Goldfish darted through the green plastic fronds, scattering the striped yellow and black fish. The blue-and-orange clown fish floated along, seeming not to notice the crazy flashes of gold. "Perhaps we should discuss something other than work."

"What would that be? Our upbringings?" She bit her lip. "Mark, face it. We don't have anything to talk about."

"I disagree. I'm very interested in your upbringing, especially since I didn't know anything about you until a month ago. When you say I've had thirty years to get to know you, you're mistaken."

"What do you know about me already?" She knew he'd had her investigated. She remembered the conversation she'd heard between him and Gloria the day she'd gone to CoCo to refuse the challenge. Their harsh words and indictment of her mother had changed her mind about competing.

A decision she'd made rashly and had regretted ever since.

"I know you're a professor in business at the University of Illinois at Chicago. I know you're single and have an apartment at the end of Rush Street." He smiled. "An interesting location, but I don't know what to make of it."

"It came available five years ago. Being in the midst of all the bars and fun appealed to me then."

The waitress set their soup in front of them. "Crab Rangoon out in minute." She hastened away.

"And now?" Mark asked.

She tasted her soup. "It's far enough away from UIC I feel like I've left work, but it's convenient to the El, making transportation easy. I'm ten floors up, so the noise doesn't keep me awake at night, and it's a well-policed neighborhood."

"I'll bet."

She grinned. "You didn't party in college?"

"Sure, I did."

She smiled to herself as she finished her soup, unable to picture him at a fraternity toga party. He struck her as so serious. "I'd like to move to a house one day. Right now, there's no need. What about you? Where do you live?"

"I have a place at Jennings."

"Jennings Towers? The new condos?" Leanne whistled. "I've heard they have a lot of square footage for a location in the city." *Pricey, too.* But then, he could afford it. Another difference in their upbringings.

Mark finished his soup and set his bowl to the side with hers. As though this had been a prearranged signal, the waitress plunked down two small plates, a serving platter of crab Rangoon and a bowl of red sauce, then whisked their bowls away.

"I could use her at Collins," Mark said, staring after the

woman as she made a speedy crossing of the room. "She could help Mrs. Pickett."

Leanne bit into the crisp fried appetizer and almost moaned. Filled with cream cheese and spices, it contained chunks of genuine crabmeat. Her lids dropped as she took another bite. "This is delicious."

Mark's eyes darkened to a deep rich brown. "I can tell."

"How? You haven't had any yet."

He shifted in his seat. "That's okay. I'll just watch you eat yours."

Leanne set the last tidbit on her plate. She cleared her throat, feeling heat wash over her face. "I enjoy good food."

"I didn't mean to embarrass you." His white teeth gleamed in his smile. Her heart stuttered.

He's your nephew. The cold, mean voice in her head had her looking away. Remind him of your relationship, she thought. Remind yourself. "What was it like growing up a Collins?"

His smile disappeared. He glanced over her shoulder, but the little waitress didn't come running with their entrees. "Normal, I guess."

"I don't know anything about your father, even though he's my half-brother. Are you like him or more like Gloria?"

"My father, I guess. I was raised to head up Collins, so I'm more business-minded than my mother."

Leanne hunched her shoulders. Again she felt the pangs of how unfair this competition was to Mark.

"Sorry if that makes you uncomfortable," he said, "but it's a fact."

Her expression must have given away her thoughts. She'd have to watch that in the business world. If she had the chance to worry about it.

The waitress brought their food, and they portioned out their servings without talking. The red peppers in the Hunan chicken burned her throat and had her reaching for water.

"What will you do when I win?" she asked.

Mark drew back, blinked, and then laughed. "You mean after rushing my mother to the E.R.?"

Leanne smiled. "Gloria will have a fit."

He shook his head. "Gloria will have a heart attack." He raised his teacup. "Here's to a fair fight."

She raised her cup and extended it toward his.

"May the best man win," he said.

Clink. The forward motion tapped her cup against his as his words registered.

"Hey!" She snatched back her hand.

Mark chuckled, and she couldn't help joining him.

"You're a sneak."

"I'm a Collins."

She absorbed that for a moment. The longer she didn't respond, the worse the comment sounded. "Does that mean it won't be a fair fight?"

"I meant it as a joke, Leanne. I won't knowingly make the competition any more unfair than it already is."

She narrowed her eyes at him. "Why? What have you done?"

"You mean besides running the company since the Lion's death? Or working there all my life? Getting all that insider knowledge you don't have?" He tossed down a bite of Mongolian beef. "Not a thing."

She winced. "Sorry. I don't know you, but I do know big business. It can be cutthroat."

Mark blew out his breath. "I tend to get upset when someone questions my integrity."

After a moment his lips twitched. Her breath caught in her throat. She could picture them being friends. She'd lose that friendship as soon as the contest ended, no matter the outcome. She didn't want to get close to him when it would end badly. Nevertheless, excitement shivered over her skin.

"I'll remember that," she said. "No cracks about your integrity. Wouldn't want to break your heart."

"Hey, just because I'm a Collins doesn't mean I don't have a heart. Must have gotten it from my real parents."

Leanne froze. "Your what?"

Chapter Four

"My real parents," Mark said, looking at her quizzically. "My biological ones, I mean. Gloria and Warren are my real parents, of course."

She swallowed, unable to form words. Words? She could barely breathe. "You're adopted?"

"I thought you knew."

She shook her head, overwhelmed.

Mark shrugged. "It's not a secret. My mother—Gloria, I mean—couldn't conceive. Adoption was the only answer for her and my father. Warren."

This time she nodded to show she understood. But while she followed his explanation, she didn't understand at all. How could she have not known? Did her mom know?

We're not related by blood? Possibilities rose to her mind. To tear herself away from images of she and Mark getting more intimately involved, she asked, "Is that why you call Gloria by her first name?"

"Kids call their parents whatever they're taught to call them." He took a bite of chicken.

Leanne stared at her plate but couldn't imagine trying to swallow right then. Her throat knotted against the idea.

"When I asked about why I was brought up to call them by their first names," he went on, "they said it never occurred to them to have me call them anything else. I tried calling them 'Mother' and 'Father,' but they seemed more comfortable being 'Gloria' and 'Warren.'" He shrugged, as if it were no big deal.

Leanne nodded and stirred her tea before realizing she hadn't added anything to stir. She set the spoon aside, hoping Mark hadn't noticed. *It's okay that I find him attractive*, she thought with relief. She glanced at him again. *Attractive* didn't begin to express her opinion of his appearance.

His face hardened. "Don't be thrown by this. I'm a Collins. Not by blood, maybe, but I've earned my way into this family."

Perplexed and still reeling with the implications of his adoption on their possible future relationship, she said, "You don't earn your way into a family."

"You do if you're not born into one."

"That's not how it works, Mark."

He crossed his arms on the table and glowered at her. "How would you know anything about it? You're not adopted."

She stared at him, a disbelieving laugh caught on that knot in her throat. "You think being born with Lionel's blood in me made me a Collins?"

He flushed.

"Go talk to your mother," she said.

"What do you mean by that?"

"You know perfectly well. It's no secret how she feels. How any of you feel about me. I'm thirty years old, Mark, and in that thirty years, not one member of the Collins family has ever contacted me."

"I didn't know about you."

"But Gloria did. I'm betting your father—my half-brother—" she emphasized "—did. Lionel certainly knew about me. But other than sending checks, he couldn't be bothered. I'm sure he had his secretary write them."

"What checks?"

Leanne slumped back in her chair. She hadn't meant to mention the money. "Lionel sent monthly checks. My mom sees them as a testament to his love for us."

"Sees them? Are they still coming?"

She nodded. "Up till his death. I've banked them for my children. An inheritance. I thought about returning them, but why should I? Lionel was rich. My kids, at least, should benefit from that."

She watched the fish swim futilely in their tank. Around they went, through the plastic grass, past the fake rock formations.

"How do you see them?"

Trapped.

"Leanne?"

She blinked and focused on Mark. "What?"

"How do you view the checks the Lion sent?"

"Oh." Picking up her fork, she stirred through the Hunan chicken. "It's conscience money, although alleging Lionel had scruples is a stretch for me. It's payoff, but don't tell my mother that."

"Why not?" He speared a piece of beef.

Leanne tore her gaze from his lips as they closed around the fork. *Not my nephew* kept beating against her temples like tribal drums. Should she dance or circle the wagons? She ate something off her plate trying to appear in control. Unfortunately, she couldn't fool herself. "Mom wouldn't listen. She thinks he loved her."

"Can I ask a question without you biting my head off?"

She frowned. "What do you mean?"

"You're a bit defensive, especially when it comes to your mother."

"What about my mother?" Leanne heard her tone and had to laugh. "Yeah, I guess I am. Sorry. I just know how your family feels about her. It's natural, and I understand it. I just don't want her hurt by the Collins animosity."

With precise movements, he set his fork by his plate and locked his gaze on hers.

She gulped.

"First of all," he said, "I am not my family. I am a man who knew nothing of you or your mother."

She nodded when he paused.

"Secondly, I didn't experience 'the Collins animosity' nor do I feel it now that I know about you two. I'm not saying my family didn't have hard feelings toward your mother. I'm just saying I never saw or heard about it."

"Okay." Leanne figured he must have been oblivious, not knowing the situation. He'd been young at the time of the affair, but she didn't think the family just forgot about it. The way Gloria treated her now, as though she were spit on the sidewalk, Leanne knew there'd been more than "hard feelings."

But she understood Mark's meaning. She shouldn't tar

him with the same brush as the rest of the Collinses. She drew a breath, preparing for something unpleasant. Anything Mark hesitated over saying would no doubt get her back up. "So, what did you want to ask?"

"This is in the line of getting to know you, okay? Not an attack on your mom."

Again she nodded. It must be bad.

"Was she involved with other men when you were little?"

Count to ten, she told herself. One, he warned you you wouldn't like the question. Two, there was no nasty insinuation her mom went from man to man. Three— She popped her purse, located her wallet. Four, drew out a ten-dollar bill and tossed it on the table.

"Wait. What are you—?"

Five, stood, glared. Six, spun and stalked away, head high, not giving him a word.

At least she'd made it to two.

Mark snapped his mouth shut. If he'd kept it shut, he'd still be getting to know Leanne. Well, he'd found out one thing; she had a temper.

But, dammit, he'd told her he didn't mean to insinuate anything by it before he posed the question. Growling under his breath, he got his wallet, found only a one and some twenties. He laid a twenty beside her ten and pushed back his chair. The waitress would no doubt be thrilled to get a forty-eight percent tip. Efficiency should be rewarded, but this was ridiculous.

Mark caught sight of the waitress scurrying toward him and quickened his step. She nearly vaulted over a table to stop in front of him.

Her ageless face had folded into creases. "Food no good? Sick?"

"The food was fine. We enjoyed it very much."

Her face smoothed out. "Want box? Take home?"

"No, I'm sorry, we're going to work. No way to keep it cold." Except the refrigerator in his office's bar. It would be good later, and he hadn't finished.

Jeez, what was he thinking? He stepped around the small woman. "I have to catch her. We're sharing a cab."

"Come again."

"Sure, sure." As though he'd ever get another date with Leanne. Not that this had been a date.

When he opened the restaurant door, he caught the blur of her racing down the sidewalk. She stalked along with her head up, like a queen. *Yeah, a drama queen.* The impact of her high heels could have cracked divots out of the concrete. Keeping his stride at just under a run, Mark caught up with her. He thought to grasp her arm, to slow or stop her, but figured she'd roundhouse-punch him with the other fist. Law of averages made her right-handed, so he stepped to that side and kept pace. If he was going to get hit, he'd rather it be with her weaker arm.

Her clenched jaw and scowl warned him to tread carefully.

"I told you I didn't mean anything by it," he all but accused her. Crap, wrong tone. He tried again. "I'm sorry you were upset, but I wasn't being nasty."

"My mother never even dated," she spat out, as though against her will. At least she was talking to him.

"I told you, I just wanted to know what your life was like growing up. Did you have a father figure or male role model or whatever the shrinks call it these days? It wasn't a slam against your mom." He chanced a touch to her elbow, keeping a weather eye on her fists.

Leanne halted in the middle of the sidewalk, perhaps unaware of the people pushing past them, muttering about inconsiderate so-and-sos. Mark ignored them, concentrating on her. Watching her as her breathing slowed, her lips relaxed, her eyes lost their fury.

After a few minutes had passed, Leanne sighed. "Okay, I'm sorry I bit your head off."

He smiled as she echoed his earlier phrase.

"Mom never dated," she repeated.

"Never? That's incredible. I believe you," he rushed on, seeing her eyes narrow. "It's just she's so…lively. That's not the right word. Friendly?" He shook his head, gave it up. "What about after you were grown?"

"Not even then."

"Why do you think she didn't date?"

She shrugged. "It only dawned on me she didn't when I started dating, but by then I was a teenager. I couldn't ask something so personal."

He grinned. "Because she might ask something personal in return?"

"There's that, and because I didn't want to hurt her."

"Touché." He dipped his head in salute for her dig at him. "How could you not notice she wasn't dating?"

Leanne took a few steps before she answered. Slow, easy steps, thank God. Mark glanced at the street, saw no unengaged taxis, and gave a mental shrug.

"We had our own world," she finally said, "complete with just the two of us. We did everything together. Pals, as well as mother and daughter." She shrugged. "It didn't seem like anything was missing."

"Like a man?"

She nodded.

"Ready for another hard question?"

She rolled her eyes, a glint of humor shading her mouth. "You're a risk-taker, and not just in business."

He chuckled, relieved she'd put away her pointed hat and broom. "Did she not date because she loved the Lion or because she hated him? Because he'd treated her badly."

"Oh, she loved him. Without doubt. Still does."

"Even though he abandoned her when she became pregnant?"

"Even though he abandoned her when he got her pregnant, you mean?"

"Uh, right."

"Mark, my mom knew he wouldn't leave his family. We've had lots of talks about this. She knew she was second-place. But she loved him, and she's sure he loved her, truly, deeply loved her."

"What do you think?"

Leanne shrugged. "I don't know. I wasn't there."

"Well…"

She looked over and with a half-laugh, she relaxed. "Okay, maybe I was around there at the end, but I didn't know him. Did he seem to you like the kind of man to have an affair with someone he didn't love?"

Mark stilled and blanked his expression. Crap. Why'd she have to ask that?

"Mark?"

"I think I see a taxi." He sidestepped, hoping she'd

think he just hadn't heard her question. In line with his luck today, the taxis all had passengers, but he raised his arm, waved, and kept up the pretense.

"What?" When he remained silent, she asked again. "What aren't you telling me?"

He glanced her way, then quickly back to the street.

"If we're going to get to know one another," she said, "we need total honesty."

He lowered his arm and looked her in the eye. Taking a deep breath, he braced himself for her reaction. "My mother thinks the Lion had several affairs."

Leanne felt her face drain of blood.

"I'm sorry," Mark said in a gentle voice. "Gloria's sure his relationship with your mother was the last. She's positive there aren't any other children."

"I didn't think of that. Other children." Tears pricked, and she squeezed her eyes shut. She would not cry. She would not. Her mother would be devastated if she learned she'd been only one of many of Lionel's conquests, not the love of his life.

Of course, her mother knew she'd shared his affection with his wife. She just didn't know she'd shared with anyone else. *Oh, God.*

Leanne wanted to flee, but she'd already done that today. She couldn't retreat, not in front of Mark. Feeling exposed, she put her hands over her face. "Give me a minute."

She felt him take a half step back and just hoped he'd found some interesting architecture to study rather than her.

She drew a breath, trying to steady herself. Her mother

viewed her relationship with Lionel through rosy clouds, making the liaison more romantic. Now it seemed sordid.

Several affairs. Did Mark think his assurance that there were no other bastards like her running around would make her feel better?

She'd never *felt* like a bastard before. She'd merely been illegitimate. All her life, she'd been told she was the result of an overwhelming love. She'd tried to believe it. Since her mother had loved Lionel, Leanne had thought of herself as conceived from that love, even if only one of her parents had felt it. Wanted, cherished, rejoiced in. Now she knew her mother had been used, and it left her feeling unclean as well.

She wiped tears from her eyes. Never again would she cry over Lionel Collins. Never again would she give anyone from that family the power to hurt her.

She squared her shoulders and met Mark's concerned gaze.

"Sorry," she forced out.

"Don't be. I shouldn't have told you."

"The truth hurts." She tried to smile, but felt it wobble on her lips. "I'm better off knowing."

Mark just looked at her, neither agreeing nor disagreeing.

"I'm not usually so emotional. Our lunch today has been like riding on a roller coaster. Up and down."

"At least there was an up."

"Don't forget the screaming."

He smiled.

Leanne stepped to the curb, put her fingers in her mouth and blew a piercing whistle. She saw Mark's mouth drop just as a cab pulled to her side.

"How the hell did you do that?" His tone held awe.

"I coached a girls' soccer team for five years." She got in the cab, grinning at his expression. They could have walked to the Collins Company, but she didn't think her legs would carry her.

He slid in. "Do you have a daughter?"

She laughed. "No. There just aren't enough coaches in the YMCA program. I told them if they had a rule book and a video, I'd take on a team."

"But no one asked you to do it? A neighbor? An overworked friend?" He spoke as though she'd just landed from Jupiter. And might zoom back home at any moment.

His reaction lightened her spirits considerably. "One of my grad students told me he coached, so I looked into it. I got more out of it than I gave, believe me."

He shook his head, a smile working the corners of his lips. "Another thing I never knew about you."

Something the private detective didn't have in his report? she wanted to say. Leanne would bet ten bucks Gloria knew all kinds of things about her. "Thank you, Mark, for being honest with me. I guess Lionel's swearing off affairs after being with my mom is another reason your mother hates me." She tried to be glib. "It shows how important my mom was to him."

He cocked his head. "What do you mean, another reason?"

She ticked them off on her fingers. "I'm stealing part of your inheritance by taking the money Lionel left me. I'm competing against you for CEO of CoCo. I refused to take her up on her offer to buy me off. I'm—"

"Her what?" he cut in.

Leanne looked at him, distracted from recounting her sins as seen by Gloria. "Her offer to buy me off. Your offer, too, I guess."

He stared at her, his lips a flat line.

"That first envelope?" she reminded him. "The day the board laid out the rules of the competition?"

"I have no idea what you're talking about."

She hesitated. He seemed sincere. Was he playing her, or had he really not known? "The second envelope was from Lionel, as yours was."

He nodded. "I've wondered what he wrote."

"'You have the Collins blood in you. My blood,'" she quoted. "'Here's your chance at the Collins fortune.' Quite dramatic."

Mark's gaze stayed on his clenched hands. "And the other envelope?"

"As you know, it contained an offer, signed by Gloria, to pay me five million dollars if I'd forget I ever heard the name Collins, in business or personally."

Mark clenched his fists tighter, striving to control his emotions. He couldn't believe his mother had done this. Okay, he could, but he didn't want to. Gloria knew he didn't want her to use her inheritance from Lionel to pave his way. He'd said that to her in so many words.

"It didn't actually say, 'Be out of town by sundown,'" Leanne said, "but that's the gist of it."

He couldn't believe—

Mark swore under his breath. He knew damned good and well Gloria was capable of doing whatever she deemed necessary to protect the family. In this case, that included saving the Collins Company. "I'm sorry."

"You really didn't know?"

"No." His back teeth locked, and he had to force himself to unclench them before he could continue. "I didn't know. I told her not to offer to buy you off."

The cab pulled to the curb.

She beamed and thrust open the door, crawling out of the taxi. "How did you know I wouldn't take it?"

Mark closed his eyes. Leanne looked so pleased that he'd believed in her, or read her so well, or whatever she thought. But he hadn't been acting out of honor. He'd been pissed off and unwilling to pay for something he felt he had a right to already.

But he couldn't tell her that. She'd hate him.

"Seven-forty," the cab driver said. At Mark's scowl, he said, "We got a minimum, bud."

Mark threw the guy a twenty—he'd have to get some smaller bills—and waited for change. Unable to stall any longer, he forced himself out after Leanne.

He glanced at her, then quickly away. Her smile faltered on her lips.

He should tell her something, even if it were a bit short of the whole truth. This wasn't a freaking court of law, after all. "I wasn't positive you'd turn it down since we'd just met."

"Then why tell her not to do it?"

The pleased expression had vanished from her eyes now too, leaving her guarded. He wanted to say something to put that look back on her face. For a second, he thought she'd come close to regarding him as a decent person.

Losing her good opinion bothered him more than he wanted it to—which was not at all.

"It's pretty good advice," she said with an edge to her tone. "You never know, I might have been tempted by that much money. Then you wouldn't be in this stupid competition with me. Your place at CoCo wouldn't be in jeopardy."

He opened his mouth, then snapped it shut on words that would surely enrage her. He hoped she hadn't noticed.

She had. He could tell by her narrowed eyes. "But, of course, you don't consider your place at CoCo to be in jeopardy, do you? What threat am I, a mere teacher?"

Her creamy complexion flashed past pink to bright red faster than he could distinguish the shades. Her good opinion of him vanished even quicker. He knew it by the heat in her eyes, the set of her jaw. Any chance they'd had to be—

To be what? he wondered. Family? Not likely. Friends?

His mind closed against the whisper saying they could have been more. Legally, morally, ethically, there was no problem. They weren't blood relatives. They were strangers.

The problem was they shared a past. Or, more accurately, they hadn't shared a past, since she'd been ignored and left unacknowledged by his family.

He watched her stiff form walk away from him. The problem was she despised him.

And he didn't despise her at all.

"Mom, why didn't you tell me Mark was adopted?" Leanne yelled down the hall. She slammed her purse onto her mother's sofa, watching as it bounced onto the floor. Figured. Her cell phone had probably just broken. Her compact mirror had no doubt cracked, bringing more bad luck. It had been that kind of day.

Her mom wiped her hands on her jeans as she came in from the kitchen. The pine scent drifting from that direction spoke of her cleaning efforts. "What are you talking about?"

"He's adopted. And you let me go on and on about how handsome he was. Didn't it occur to you I was upset about being attracted to him? To my nephew?"

Her mother cocked her head and said nothing.

After a moment, Leanne slumped onto the couch. "You didn't know."

"No." Her mom perched on the cushion next to her. "I had no idea. Which, come to think of it, I wouldn't. They would have already adopted him by the time I met Lionel."

"He never mentioned it?"

Her mother shrugged. "He said he had a grandson. His family was an uncomfortable subject for us."

Yeah, I'll bet.

They sat silently, each lost in her own thoughts.

"Did you ever think he'd leave her?" Leanne asked.

"No, I didn't want to break up his marriage. The love I had for Lionel just swept me off my feet. I never thought I'd get involved with a married man. By the time he told me, I'd already fallen. Hard."

Leanne gaped at her. "You didn't know he was married at first? I've never heard this before."

"Of course I didn't know. Lee, what a question."

"Sorry, Mom," she muttered.

Her mom shrugged. "I fought it, but he was charming. He pursued me, and I'd never been pursued, like a treasure at the end of a quest."

Leanne grimaced, not sure that was a good thing. It sounded obsessive. "Did you try to see him? After?"

"No. I sent him a card informing him of your birth. I mentioned I'd named you after him." She grinned lopsidedly. "Checks started coming in your name, so I know he got the note."

"Or had detectives find out about me."

"He didn't need to. I let him know."

Leanne hesitated over her next question. They'd talked about Lionel all her life. Her mother had never hidden anything from her. But when she was younger, she didn't have the same questions. Now her mom seemed open to a more personal discussion. "Did it hurt that he never came?"

"Yes. Oh, yes. I knew it was for the best, but I wanted him to see you. To hold you. Just once."

"It wouldn't have made any difference."

"Not in the outcome. We wouldn't have gotten back together, but I would have felt he was more a part of your life. That he could picture you, think about you. I wanted that connection, some kind of bond."

"You didn't keep him updated, did you?" Leanne asked, horrified at the idea. Surely he hadn't been keeping tabs on her from a distance?

"No, I didn't. I wanted him to get in touch if he wanted to, not be forced by my stalking him." She took Leanne's hands in hers. "I'm sorry. He never contacted me again, other than sending a check each month. I cashed a few when you were first born, while I couldn't work, then put everything else in the bank for you."

Unsettled, Leanne couldn't shake the feeling of having been watched all these years. "Do you think he hired detectives to keep an eye on me?"

"I'm sorry, Lee, but I don't believe he did." Her mom put an arm around her and squeezed her close. "I know I deprived you of your father, but there was no acceptable alternative. If I'd taken him to court, it would only have caused a scandal. I couldn't risk losing you."

"Thank God for that. I didn't want him checking up on me, personally or through a private detective or security company. That'd be creepy."

Her mom nodded, shoulders relaxing. "We'll never know."

Leanne didn't care for that answer either but acknowledged the truth of it. Gloria might know, but Leanne doubted she'd get a straight answer from her. For her own peace of mind, she'd believe Lionel had regarded her as a monthly payoff and that ended it.

Her mom sighed long and deep. She peeked at Leanne and blinked. "Does this change things? Mark being adopted?"

"Change what?"

"I don't know. Your feelings."

"Feelings?" At her mother's knowing look, Leanne shook her head. "Don't even go there. I'm not feeling anything toward Mark except rivalry. We both want the same thing. He's in my way."

"Really, Leanne? Do you want CoCo?"

Leanne searched her conscience for the truth. She came up with, "He doesn't think I deserve it. That ticks me off."

"So if you win, it's just to spite him?"

"And Gloria."

Her mom nodded. "Okay. Victory. Then what?"

Leanne studied her fingers, but had no response. Even after her mother headed back to the kitchen, she hadn't come up with an answer.

MARK GLARED as his mother stepped into his office. "What are you doing here, Gloria?"

She clicked the door shut and slid into the black leather armchair facing his desk. She crossed one leg over the other, pulled her navy skirt approximately one-sixteenth of an inch down to cover her knee, positioned her purse on the front of his desk, then patted her perfectly smooth hairdo into place on the back of her neck.

Mark growled under his breath at her deliberate stall tactics. "I don't have time for this. As charming as it always is to see you, I can't visit right now."

She showed her teeth in what others might have mistaken for a smile. "As you well know, I'm not here to visit. Don't be patronizing. What do you plan to tell the board?"

"Exactly what I told you last night. The thing CoCo needs is—"

She raised a hand. "CoCo?"

He bit back a sigh. Why did she have to be difficult today, when he especially didn't need a confrontation? "Collins, Mother. Collins needs Kellco, Art Keller's company. That's what I intend to tell the board."

"But, Mark, you know Art Keller won't have anything to do with Collins. He hated Lionel's way of doing business, and you're just like the Lion."

This time, Mark did sigh as he rested back against his

burgundy leather executive chair. "Kellco is what Collins needs. This answer will win the first task."

"And if the second task is dependent on the first?"

"Then Leanne can't win the second task any more than I can. Keller won't meet with us." He shrugged. "Every board member is well aware of the best solution to this task. I've thought of other answers, but Art Keller is it. I can't go in there with less than the best, no matter what Leanne comes up with. They'll know I've backed away from Kellco."

His mother shook her head. "You'll lose."

Mark grimaced. He didn't need her lack of faith in him pointed out right now. "Lovely to see you, Mother, but I have to go present this plan to the board." He stalked out the door, barely restraining the impulse to slam it behind him. A son should show some respect.

He entered the boardroom five minutes early to discover the others had already arrived. A stagnant silence hung over the room. The panel once again situated themselves across the table, just like on the TV show.

Mark ran his gaze over Leanne, appearing composed and too pretty. Her green jacket reminded him of shady forests and quiet paths leading to cool streams. A picnic with Leanne would be nice. Somewhere quiet, just the two of them.

They could get to know one another, away from Collins and their families. He could atone for the things he'd said getting out of the taxi. Not that he believed any differently now, but maybe he could state his views in a way that wouldn't infuriate her. Perhaps she'd stop regarding him as a monster.

Mulvany cleared his throat. "Shall we begin?"

Mark snapped his attention back to the boardroom. With Kellco as his answer to task one, he'd probably lose this round. Leanne didn't need more of an advantage, and his daydreaming about winning her good opinion wasn't helping him any.

Although why her good opinion should matter, he had no idea.

Chapter Five

Leanne nodded, her throat too tight to speak. She would lose this round. There could be no other outcome. Mark had the experience and knowledge of the company. She'd just have to endure the meeting with dignity.

Dammit.

"Would you care to start, Ms. Fairbanks?" Mulvany asked. His smile held pity, which Leanne considered a good thing. It braced her backbone as she presented her idea in the airless room. She proposed the takeover of Accessories, Inc., a company nearing bankruptcy, which made small office supplies. Its facilities and avenues of distribution would strengthen the Mark of Excellence brand. The takeover wouldn't make a huge difference in the Collins' profit/loss column, but it was her only idea.

She'd been daydreaming about Mark and fiddling with the stapler on her desk when inspiration had struck. Increasing the line of his ideas galled her, but she held her voice steady as she presented the data. With an inward sigh, she reclaimed her seat.

"Thank you, Ms. Fairbanks," Mulvany said. "Mark?"

Mark stood and made eye contact with each panel member in turn before he started. "I'm sure you all know the best solution for the Collins Company as well as I do. While the takeover of Accessories, Inc., is inspired, and I congratulate Leanne on her research—"

Leanne cut him a look from the corner of her eye. The patronizing swine.

"We all know which company Collins needs to acquire. You're also aware it is impossible."

Leanne noted the others nodding in agreement. What had she missed in her frantic search of CoCo's holdings?

"I offer it as the solution to this task, however, simply because it would be the best answer. Please don't believe I consider it the only solution or even a viable one. But, hypothetically speaking, Collins needs to acquire Kellco."

Mark resumed his seat while Leanne feverishly flipped through folders in her mind. She couldn't place the name, although it sounded familiar. She pictured the papers on her desk, full of information. Where in her research of Collins had she come across that company?

Mulvany conferred with Mr. Garland and Mrs. Metcalf in low voices. The men wore almost identical gray pin-striped suits with stiff white shirts and charcoal ties. Mrs. Metcalf wore a black pantsuit with neat pearl stud earrings. Leanne made a mental note to break out her pastels and tie-dyes.

She couldn't hear their discussion and gave it up. They'd tell her soon enough what she'd missed. She turned to study Mark, the rat, who'd used his knowledge of the company to such good purposes.

He lounged in his chair, totally at ease, looking exquisite in a three-piece navy suit with a powder-blue shirt and patterned tie. His hair swept the collar of his shirt. Her fingers itched to straighten the strands falling over his eye.

As though he'd read her mind—or become conscious of her scrutiny—Mark raked the errant lock back into place. She indulged herself long enough to watch his strong fingers complete their task. With a quiet thrill of unwanted awareness, she forced her attention back to matters at hand. Not his hand, she thought as she stole another glance at him, but the important matters.

Mulvany adjusted his tie, which had lain perfectly straight before his attentions. *A nervous gesture?* It gave Leanne pause. Why would the head of the panel be nervous? She glanced at each board member but none met her eye. Mark sat upright.

Mulvany cleared his throat. "We declare Mark Collins the winner of this round." The panel turned away again in private discussion.

Leanne held herself still, trying to show no reaction. She'd known the outcome before entering the room. She pictured her mother, full of calm dignity, at Lionel's gravesite. Leanne held the image in her mind as she turned to Mark and inclined her head. "Congratulations."

His face showed his surprise. "Thank you."

He didn't squirm, but Leanne sensed his discomfort. She'd taught enough seminars in Interview Preparation to read his body language.

He leaned toward her. "It wasn't exactly fair to you," he said in a low voice, "coming in late as you did. I really do admire your work on Accessories, Inc. That wasn't BS."

"Thank you." Leanne smiled warmly, acknowledging the sincerity of his compliment.

"I'd like to look it over and see if we could implement your plan."

Leanne froze. The audacity of the man. "You mean when you become CEO?"

He gaped at her.

"Don't you think that rather presumptuous? You've only won this round."

His mouth tightened for a moment. "No matter which of us wins, it's a good idea. One of us should pursue it."

He turned away from her, and Leanne wished she could creep out of the room unnoticed. He'd tried to be nice, and she'd antagonized him. Why did she always feel petty when they argued? She shrank from the memory of stalking out of the Chinese restaurant. Jeez. He'd invited her out as a friendly gesture. No doubt he'd been as uncomfortable as she, but she'd let emotion get the better of her.

Just then, Mulvany turned toward them. "The next task is, unfortunately, tied to this one."

Mark swore under his breath. Leanne narrowed her eyes. What was going on? Clearly everyone knew something but her.

"Due to past attempts, we realize Kellco won't meet with the Collins Company. The second task may be a wash for both of you. Therefore, we will judge your efforts as well as the outcome."

Mulvany held a piece of paper in front of him and read silently. He glanced at Mark, then shifted his gaze to Leanne. "You both must now proceed with the plan of the winner of round one. In other words, you must set up a meeting with Art Keller, owner and CEO of Kellco, to discuss buying him out and taking over his company."

Leanne stilled. Had she heard right?

"Is that all?" Mark asked in a stiff tone, with an edge of sarcasm Leanne didn't understand.

"Yes. Whichever of you gets a meeting, wins."

Mark pushed back his seat and left the room.

Leanne sat stunned, as the board members filed out of the room. Art Keller? It couldn't be.

"ART KELLER?" Leanne's mom exclaimed with a smile. "The Art Keller you've been meeting with about the internships?"

"Isn't it amazing?" Leanne set utensils on the table. Her mom had come to dinner at her apartment. They usually met at her mom's, but Leanne wanted to cook. To celebrate. Although she'd lost round one, she felt she had an edge now.

"When Mark said Kellco, I didn't connect it. I was concentrating on the research I'd done on CoCo, not even thinking of school. The name didn't click until they mentioned Mr. Keller."

"Have you called him? Set up a meeting? Does Mark know? What did he say?"

"Slow down, Mom. I can't answer everything at once." She moved the pansies she used as a centerpiece—until they died from lack of light or water, anyway, as she wasn't a very good gardener—to the empty side of her small table. "Mark has no idea of my relationship with Mr. Keller. I'm hosting a party to introduce the graduating students to prominent business owners. This would be the perfect opportunity to let Mr. Keller know of my connection to CoCo."

"Darling, that's—"

The intercom buzzed, curtailing whatever her mother thought of the idea. Leanne crossed to the door. "Yes?"

"Leanne? This is Mark. Mark Collins."

She gasped and shot a panicked glance at her mother, who had covered her mouth with a hand.

"I should have called," he continued. "Can I come up? I realize you might have plans—"

Leanne hit the buzzer, cutting him off, but unable to find words to answer him. "What's he doing here?" she hissed.

"I guess we'll find out in a minute."

"How did he get my address?"

"Lee! Snap out of it."

She jumped, startled at her mother's sharp tone. No doubt she'd heard the rising hysteria in Leanne's voice, too.

"He's coming up here in a second, and you've got cobwebs in your brain. He could have gotten your address from personnel."

"Human resources," Leanne said quietly. She shook herself. "Right." She darted a critical eye across the room. What would Mark think of her place? The living room and kitchenette were small; the magenta suede furniture comfy rather than expensive or even fashionable. Flowers didn't dominate the room, unlike some of her women friends' places, but it probably looked more girly than his apartment. And definitely more shabby.

Her doorbell rang, and she had no more time to worry about the differences in their lifestyles. If he'd come slumming, he'd have to deal with what he found.

She opened the door and stepped back to let him enter. He had finger-combed his hair, probably disheveled from the Chicago wind. Attired in chinos and a butter-soft yellow oxford shirt, he looked delicious. Probably his idea of casual clothes. She greeted him in her Field Museum T-shirt featuring Sue the T-Rex and worn jeans. Just perfect.

"Oh, Ms. Fairbanks," he said to her mother. "I didn't know you were here. Am I interrupting something?"

"Don't be silly. And, please, call me Jenny." She shook his proffered hand, which made Leanne smile. Her mom was a hugger, not a hand-shaker. She no doubt wanted Mark to feel at ease. He didn't strike her as a hugger, though.

An immediate picture of him taking her into his arms flashed into her mind. She shook her head, angry at herself. She had to get over this fascination with him. They were opponents, combatants, vying for the same prize.

"So, why are you here?" Leanne could have bitten her tongue. The words had burst out without thought. She shook her head at her unintended rudeness. The man made her nerves ragged. "I mean, would you like a drink? Please sit down." She motioned toward the couch.

Mark hesitated, then sat on the edge of the cushion. She smiled to herself. Although old and sagging, the couch wouldn't swallow him whole.

Her mother sat in the armchair across from him, pleasant anticipation on her face.

"No, thanks, I'm fine. I don't want to intrude."

Then you should have stayed away.

"Nonsense," her mother said. "You're family."

Leanne closed her mouth on a retort that would have earned her a tongue-lashing.

"Uh, thank you," Mark said, clearly disconcerted himself. "That's kind of you." His gaze darted her way, and Leanne had to smile. He'd drawn back into the sofa and appeared cornered, out of his depth.

Her mother often had that effect on people. It was her sweetness that threw them. They seldom expected someone as honestly charming and thoughtful as her mom to exist anymore. Her classic beauty—a blond, green-eyed Audrey Hepburn, Leanne thought—disarmed them; her genuine warmth melted their defenses.

"We were about to have dinner," her mother said into the silence. She laid a hand on Mark's. "Why don't you stay?"

Leanne gaped at her. That was pushing friendliness.

"Oh, no, I—"

"Please, we insist. Don't we, Leanne?"

Her mother's gaze bored into her. She gave an inward sigh. Had she just thought this woman sweet? "Uh, sure."

Her mom frowned at her, rebuking her for the half-hearted non-invitation, but it was the best she could do. Had David offered Goliath a seat at his table? Had the Greeks and Trojans gotten together for cake and coffee before the blood-shed?

He stayed, although the two of them were ill at ease. At her small round table, she couldn't avoid him. They passed dishes politely, while Leanne took great care not to touch him. Mark served himself tiny portions, perhaps recognizing she hadn't cooked for three. Maybe he wondered if he could swallow. Or if she could cook.

He didn't turn down glazed carrots or garden salad, although he hesitated over the green peas. *Men.*

Her mom caught her eye and twinkled back at her. "Could you pass the peas, Mark?"

He did so with visible relief. And none on his plate.

Fortunately, Leanne had made extra pork chops, thinking she and her mother would have leftovers. His plate filled even without peas. He bit into a dinner roll with noticeable pleasure.

"Not Chinese," a devil made Leanne say, "but edible."

Mark coughed and grabbed his water glass. Her mother glared at her while Leanne attempted an innocent expression.

"It's very good," he said.

Her mother filled the awkward silences with talk of books and movies, patter which she put into practice at the hair salon.

"I swear, that George Clooney needs to act more and direct less," her mom said. "Why hide that handsome face behind a camera?"

Mark's better looking.

Oh, great. As though she needed that realization with him so close she could smell the chilly Chicago wind on his clothes and a subtle soapy scent under that. She forced her thoughts back to George Clooney. "Maybe he's good at directing."

"He can direct when he's older," her mom countered.

"He'll still be good-looking."

Her mom sighed. "Yeah."

Leanne leaned toward Mark and said in a stage whisper, "My mom has a crush on George."

"So does Leanne," her mom countered.

"So does every woman in America."

"And many foreign countries."

Mark glanced back and forth, following their teasing as though at a tennis match.

The conversation rolled over the table, her mother's gentle tones lapping against Mark and Leanne's tension and washing away any awkwardness.

Leanne watched Mark's stiffness ease. Although he couldn't quite flow into their rhythm, he dropped his formal, careful mannerisms. He'd fallen under her mother's spell. She smiled to herself.

"I didn't see that movie," he replied to each of the suggestions her mother made. Leanne frowned. He never went to movies? He hadn't read any of the bestsellers her mom mentioned either. What did he do for fun?

An image of Mark entwined with a woman who looked remarkably like herself flitted into her mind. She shoved it away. The enemy, she reminded herself. He devoured companies for fun. Put gentle old fifty-somethings out of their jobs.

Eating and drinking with her rival. Leanne shook her head. What was she doing? Where was the hemlock?

The meal ended none too soon. They cleared the table, Mark toting things to the counter and generally getting in the way. Her kitchen was too small for the three of them. Heck, her apartment was too small for the three of them. He had to go.

She led them back to the living area. Would it be rude to point out the time? Leanne peeked at her watch. Seven-thirty. She could say she had papers to grade. Even professors could use that excuse. But on a Friday night? How pathetic did she want to appear?

"Well," her mom said, "I hate to cut the evening short, Lee, but I have early appointments tomorrow."

Leanne stared at her mother. "Surely you don't."

"No, I do. I scheduled them totally forgetting about dinner tonight. Silly me."

Leanne narrowed her eyes. Silly her, indeed.

Mark said, "I should leave. Then you can stay and finish your evening together."

"I need to get my sleep," her mom said. "I wouldn't want to dye someone's hair the wrong color. You and Lee need to get better acquainted."

Her mother gathered her purse and practically ran to the door. As she pulled it closed, she paused, wiggled her eyebrows and jerked her head at Mark. Code for, you're alone now; go get him.

Leanne put her back to the door and blew out a breath. Her mother looked like an angel, but she had a bulldog's tenacity. Pasting on a smile, she took the six steps required to reach the chair across from Mark.

Now what?

Time to get "better acquainted," as her mother put it. What could they possibly talk about? His recent win over her? Her secret knowledge, which just might oust him in the next round?

"Your mom…" he started.

Leanne felt her hackles rise. "Yes? What about my mom?" So help her, if he said one condescending thing about her mother, she'd smash something over his head.

He grinned. "She's pretty amazing."

Leanne melted, returning his smile. "Yeah."

"I came in here, pretty agitated if you didn't notice, and she just made me feel…" He glanced around the room. "at home."

If only he hadn't shaken his head as if the idea of feeling at home in her small apartment had to be totally foreign. If only he didn't look so bemused by the idea. She'd almost been charmed by his smile. Almost forgot he was the enemy. "Why did you stop by?"

He started. "Oh. There's something you need to know. Something you don't know about Collins."

She narrowed her eyes. "What?" She heard the accusation in her tone, but didn't feel one bit sorry.

"Now I'm wondering why the hell I should tell you anything. I must have been crazy." He surged to his feet, and she rose to meet him.

The tension in the room could have sparked a fire. She felt it in her body, saw it in his face.

"I actually thought," he said, "it was unfair you didn't know. Hard enough for you to go through this asinine contest without any background, I told myself. It was only decent to tell you."

His indrawn breath sucked the air from the room. Her awareness of him sharpened.

"But now I see you don't need any help." He stepped toward her, into her space. She felt the heat from his body.

"What are you talking about?" Her voice, a mere thread, sounded strained even to her ears. She should step back. He wasn't angry, exactly, and she didn't fear him. But as his aggravation built, he got closer and quieter and more intense. More overpowering without threatening. More *male*.

And she was responding. Her body leaned toward his without her permission. Her blood strummed faster. Her skin tingled to be touched.

Dammit. This wasn't how warfare went.

Mark leaned in until he was practically nose-to-nose with her. "Kellco won't meet with Collins. Art Keller hated the Lion. I thought you should know that. I thought you should be aware that there is no good outcome to this task."

"Thank you," Leanne whispered. She was aware when his body relaxed, when he flowed toward her, not moving, but reaching out, male to female. Knew before he leaned forward that his kiss would scorch her. Brand her. Change her in ways she didn't want, wouldn't recognize.

She let her eyes close, not wanting to acknowledge the moment. Not wanting to stop it.

His lips closed over hers gently. Persuading.

Her stomach clenched, and she had to grab on to his shoulders so as not to fall. He didn't stop, nor did he enfold her in his arms. She didn't know she'd wanted him to until it didn't happen. But she felt the absence of his embrace, even as she felt his possession of her mouth. The contradiction stirred in her belly, slid downward.

Her fingers flexed, drawing him closer, but he didn't move. She wanted full body contact to rub away this prickling on her skin. Irritated when he wouldn't come nearer, she pulled back and broke contact with the delight of his mouth.

His brown eyes had darkened; his skin flushed. His breathing came as labored as did hers. Why was he holding back? Her mind raced through possibilities while their gazes silently dueled. She didn't care for any of the answers. Finally she broke the silence. "Are you involved with someone else?"

His expression admonished her. "I wouldn't be here…at least, not here doing this, if I were."

Then why, she wanted to cry, *won't you kiss me? Really kiss me?* She felt the potential for breath-stealing passion. Heck, she'd already had her breath stolen by just his kiss.

She stepped back. "It's CoCo."

"I can't get involved with you, Leanne, then go cut your throat in the boardroom. Some businessmen can do that, I know. I'm not that ruthless." His laugh was dry. "Yet another disappointment to the Lion."

"I see." She walked to the door then turned to look at him.

"Here's your hat, what's your hurry?" he said, mocking her. He walked over, hesitated, then left without a word.

Chapter Six

Leanne sighed over a delicious plate of fettuccini Alfredo and blamed her melancholy on spring fever. She'd missed most of April researching for the first task. Now the first week of May had slipped away, as well. She anticipated the end of this school year more eagerly than her students did. Her department chair had assigned her only one class for summer, for which she felt grateful. Then she'd only have to deal with Mark.

She scowled as she thought of him, then cleared her expression. Looking around the restaurant, she didn't think the rest of the lunch crowd had noticed. Many of the city's top business people gathered here. Comfy armchairs rolled on thick carpet to tuck the diner in under a wooden table. Cloth table covers, real silver and delicate china presented delicious food in a graceful manner. A very elegant setting for some of the throat-cutting that transpired over meals.

She glanced at Art Keller's table, relieved he hadn't left while she'd been daydreaming. It had been four days—and three very long nights—since Mark had kissed her. She'd yet to come to terms with it.

She darted a glance at the table where Mark sat with other Collins executives. Damn the man. How had he found out where and when Art Keller would be having lunch?

Probably much the same way she had, she conceded. Trickery. She'd convinced Mr. Keller's secretary she needed to confirm a last-minute detail on the party she was hosting. She told the secretary only Mr. Keller knew about this detail, a scholarship he'd promised to present to an undergrad.

No telling what Mark, the lying, kissing sneak, had told the secretary. If Art really wouldn't meet with Collins, how had Mark gotten insider info?

Mark stood, and Leanne tracked his movements from the corner of her eye. Then gasped. He couldn't be. He wouldn't approach Mr. Keller here. But he could and was. She shook her head. The guy had nerve, she'd give him that. Keller might cut him cold in front of this roomful of business people. A move like that would kill Mark's reputation and be the talk of the golf circuit for months.

Leanne narrowed her eyes. Of course he knew that. Mark was counting on Art Keller to have better manners than to do it. Ballsy move, but she doubted Mr. Keller would appreciate—or forget—being put on the spot.

Mark crossed the carpeted floor with an easy gait. If he felt nervous, she couldn't tell. His smile on reaching the table radiated charm. Keller stood, shook his hand, introduced him to the others. Not two minutes passed before Mark turned and made his way back to his own table.

A brief chat, she mused. Friendly, though. Mark's gamble had paid off. Although Keller hadn't lingered with him, neither had he slighted Mark.

Very interesting. Did that mean Mark had made progress? She'd guess so. A handshake and a few words didn't amount to much, usually, but since Keller wouldn't meet with Collins, this seemed like a small victory.

Leanne wiped her mouth and discreetly retouched her lipstick, checking for parsley in her teeth. That'd make an impression, she thought, forcing herself to relax. If Mark could approach Art Keller in front of everyone, so could she.

Mark and his party rose. Dammit. He had to see her talk to Keller. She tossed her napkin on the table and walked over to Keller's table. In her periphery, she saw Mark pause. Good. He'd spotted her. He hadn't made eye contact in the past few days, but he was, by God, noticing her now.

"Mr. Keller," she said, smiling as she approached.

Mark stalked from the room. Nothing could have made her happier.

Art Keller rose, smiling as well. In his early sixties, he remained fit. His charcoal suit lent dignity to his distinguished features. "Ms. Fairbanks." They shook hands while he introduced her to the three other gentlemen at the table.

Two held executive positions at Kellco. Leanne tagged their names and titles to their features so she could remember later. She'd jot herself a note when she got to the ladies' room.

The third man's name she recognized from her list of invitees.

"I hope you'll be able to attend the party I'm hosting," she said to Harvey Croppey. She reminded him of the details.

"I'm sure my secretary has responded," he told her, shaking her hand. "Now that I've met you, I'll double-check my calendar. See what I can do to make it." His wink and secret squeeze of her hand made it harder for Leanne to hold her smile, but she managed. Croppey's firm employed several of her former grads. His was a good connection to have.

She extricated herself and turned to Art Keller. His resemblance to Robert Redford came as a welcome sight. His face wasn't as weatherworn as the actor's and since Art spent his time in an office rather than outdoors, he also had fewer wrinkles, but the allure of his ice-blue eyes clinched it. She'd liked him at their first meeting.

"I noticed you speaking to Mark Collins," she said, watching his face. His expression remained the same, offering her no clue as to his feelings about Mark. Why couldn't the man grimace? Give her a little hope, for Pete's sake.

"I don't know if you've heard—" Although in the tight business circles of the top area companies it was likely he had. "I'm working there, in a way."

His eyebrows rose. "Working there? No, I hadn't heard that."

She caught the gleam in his eyes and smiled ruefully. "*Working there* isn't the exact term for it, I suppose."

He grinned. "From what I hear, you're staging a coup."

"No," she exclaimed, horrified. "Is that the rumor going around?"

Art took her elbow and stepped aside. In the posh restaurant, plenty of room separated the tables, giving them a semblance of privacy. "It's not as strongly phrased as that, Ms. Fairbanks. I like the idea, though. About time Collins got his comeuppance."

Leanne frowned. Lionel deserved such vindictiveness, but she didn't think Mark did. However, she couldn't argue with Art and stay in his good graces. When she didn't correct him, she felt she'd betrayed Mark.

On the other hand, how did she know Mark wasn't as much of a viper in business as Lionel had been? The rationalization sounded lame even to her.

Tough. She squared her shoulders. This was business.

"I'd like to meet with you," she ventured.

Art frowned. "To discuss the Collins Company?"

She nodded.

"I don't deal with Collins. I'm sure you know that."

"I heard you didn't deal with Lionel. You don't deal with Mark." She paused, holding his gaze.

After a moment, a smile spread across his face, then he erupted in a chuckle. He patted her arm. "Good for you, Leanne, good for you. I'll think about it."

She all but skipped back to her table. She signed her bill, thinking the extra expense of eating here well worth the cuts she'd have to make in her grocery budget this week.

He hadn't agreed to anything, she reminded herself. That he'd consider meeting with her made her feel like flying back to the university.

The next day she made her way to Mark's office. He might try to avoid her, she thought, but he wouldn't succeed. She could hardly wait to tell him about the party.

Don't gloat, she reprimanded herself. *Rise above it.*

Or gloat just a little, but don't be obnoxious. She debated the matter as Mrs. Pickett, his secretary, ushered her into his office. To heck with it. She'd let his behavior determine hers.

"Leanne," he said, rising. "I'm glad you've come by."

She stumbled a step. "Oh?"

He looked tired, though why she cared or even noticed, she didn't ask herself, certain she wouldn't like the answer. His drawn face sagged. His eyes had faint circles below them. He hadn't appeared this haggard after Lionel's funeral.

"What's going on?" she asked.

"Nothing. What makes you ask?"

"You look tired." She could have bitten her tongue out. Now he knew she noticed his appearance. And cared. Darn it. She'd never have the upper hand with him.

The conversation with Art Keller popped into her mind. Now wasn't the time to provoke him with that, though. She'd never kick a man when he was down.

"Late nights," he said.

Another image replaced Art Keller. Mark, with a slender woman in his arms. Rumpled sheets, candles, jazz playing low in the background... She banished the picture from developing further. He could enjoy a late night however he chose.

The pig.

Mark rubbed his eyes with his right hand, pinching the bridge of his nose. "I'm glad to see you."

"You said that."

"Did I?" He blinked.

Even confused, he looked adorable. Scruffy and needing care, but cute as a teddy bear. Leanne shook her head.

He scowled. "Sit down, why don't you? No sense hovering over me."

She clenched her teeth and sat in the chair facing his desk. Paper rustled in her skirt pocket.

"I saw you at the restaurant," he said.

She smiled pleasantly and waited for him to continue.

He crossed his arms over his chest. "I saw you approach Art Keller."

"And here I didn't think you'd noticed me at all this past week."

"Oh, I've noticed. Believe me." He sighed. "Let's get it out on the table, Leanne, plain and simple. I can't have an affair with you while we're in this competition."

Her breath caught in her throat. She stared at him.

"It wouldn't be right, and while that may not matter to some men, it matters to me."

"Bully for you," she muttered.

"What?"

"I said, what makes you think I'd have an affair with you? One kiss?" She forced a laugh. "You must think a lot of yourself."

Mark flushed and sat forward. "That's not what I said."

"No? You just drew the line. This side, business. That side, sex. Well, guess what? I'm not interested in stepping over that line. The business side suits me fine."

"I didn't mean sex. Not…"

She motioned for him to continue.

His mouth snapped shut. "Of course, I meant sex, but I didn't mean anything sordid."

"What makes you think I need warning off?" She leaned forward, felt the paper fold inside her pocket. Felt the heat in her face. "Did I come on to you? Corner you in the men's room? Make lewd remarks?"

"Don't be stupid."

"Now I'm stupid and sex-starved."

"Leanne." He rose.

She jumped to her feet, damned if she'd let him tower over her.

"It was all me," he said.

Leanne teetered as her fury lost force like a sailboat in a sudden calm. She caught the edge of the desk. "What?"

"It's all me. I'm the one who's attracted. To you."

"Oh. Well." She groped for the chair behind her. "Sure it's to me. What's the point if it wasn't me you're…"

"Attracted to," he finished for her.

She nodded.

"The thing is," he said as he resumed his seat, "I'm tempted to forget our situation."

She gripped her cold hands together. "That I'm Lionel's daughter?"

"No, no." He waved away the idea with a sweep of his hand. "My adoption makes that moot."

Leanne nodded. Let it be spoken, let it be done. If only things in her life were so easy. His confidence amazed her. Because it wasn't an issue to Mark, it wasn't an issue.

"So, what's the problem?" she asked. Then wanted to slap herself. Quickly, she tacked on, "Other than me not wanting an affair with you, of course."

His knowing smile had her narrowing her eyes.

"Of course," he said too smugly for her taste.

His mockery had her ire up.

"I'm sure we could work on that," he said.

His confidence had her reaching into her pocket. She withdrew the card and tossed it on his desk.

"What's this?"

"A party I'm throwing. Just a school thing to introduce business students to local business leaders." She smiled. "Art Keller will be there."

She turned as Mark's jaw dropped. Opened the door, but couldn't quite force herself out. She pivoted back. "Be sure to bring a date."

LEANNE SIPPED the spring water in her wineglass and surveyed the party. The movers and shakers of the corporate world mingled with the University of Illinois at Chicago's business students, graduates and staff. More of the top bosses from the Chicago area had shown up this year, and she had to thank Lionel for that. She knew full well they'd come to gawk at the Lion's illegitimate daughter, the woman attempting to oust Mark Collins. She tipped her glass in a toast to her father, who'd finally done one nice thing in her life. At least he was no longer zero-for-thirty-years. Not that he'd set her up in this rivalry to be nice, she thought with a mental snort.

She noted the servers threading through the crowd with appetizers. The caterer kept the buffet table of finger foods filled and the used dishes cleared. She nodded, pleased. Even the piano student from the music department had a nice selection of tunes to fill the background silence.

"Here you are, Lee," her mother said, coming up beside her. She wore an emerald cocktail dress with a handkerchief hem and hardly any back. She'd swept her blond hair up in a sophisticated twist, which exposed her elegant bare neck.

"Hope I got your genes," Leanne said. "You look gorgeous."

Her mom smiled. "So do you. That gold dress is smashing on you."

Leanne's satin dress shimmered with each movement. She gave a little twist of her waist to show her mom. "It's nice to feel feminine for a change. I never take the time when I'm working. At either place."

Her mom nodded. "I feel like I'm playing dress-up. I'm glad you invited me."

Leanne eyed her. "Even though it was like extracting an elephant's tusk to get you here?"

"I'm not sure I care for that comparison. Now that I'm here, I can't remember why I was nervous." Her mom gestured toward the room. "How do you think it's going?"

"Good." Leanne nodded, scanning the crowd. She wasn't waiting for anyone in particular to show, she told herself. Just keeping an eye on the party in her responsibility as official hostess. "The students are making their contacts. A few have already gotten invited to interviews. Jock Harding, VP at Phillips, wrote a note on the back of his card and told Melissa Jenkins to set up an appointment to interview at his company."

"A note from the VP?" Her mom blew a soundless whistle. "That won't hurt any."

Leanne smiled. "She's not the only one with that kind of story. I think the night's going well."

"The night's going extremely well," a male voice sounded from behind Leanne.

She turned and extended her hand. "Mr. Keller, how nice of you to come."

He shook her hand, but his smile had moved on to her mom. "My pleasure, Leanne. I don't believe I've met your companion."

Leanne swallowed a grin. "Mom, this is Art Keller, owner and CEO of Kellco. Mr. Keller, this is my mother, Jenny Fairbanks."

He took her mother's hand between both his, holding the handshake a smidge longer than simple politeness dictated. He turned to Leanne. "You staying on your toes with Mark the Shark?"

"Mark the what?"

"Shark. He's as ruthless as his grandfather. Eats smaller companies and the innocent for breakfast." Art turned his smile on her mom.

"I'm sure one conducts business as one deems necessary," her mother said.

Art gaped.

Leanne hid a smile as her mom set out to annihilate Art. In a gracious and polite manner, of course.

"You've heard, no doubt," her mother continued, staring right at him, "that Lionel and I were involved years ago."

"I meant no disrespect to you," Art backtracked.

"He's just recently passed. It hardly seems proper to speak ill of him when he can't defend himself."

"Believe me, I said worse to him in person."

"Hardly a thing to brag about."

Leanne fought a giggle. Her mom had on her queenly airs. Art didn't stand a chance.

"I'm sorry, Jenny," he said. "I only meant I never talk behind a man's back if I wouldn't or haven't said the same to his face."

Her mom shrugged delicately. "Most commendable."

Bringing her mom to a gathering of Lionel's friends and rivals had been a gamble. Leanne counted on the good manners of seasoned businessmen and women, much the same as Mark had when he approached Art Keller in the restaurant.

Her gaze swept the room again.

"Please accept my apology," he said. "I don't usually put my foot so far down my throat."

Her mom smiled at him. "Let's start over then." She held out her hand, which he took. "Hi, I'm Jenny."

"You don't have a drink, Jenny," he said with a smile. "Let's fix that. Can I get you anything, Leanne?"

She shook her head. "No, thank you, Mr. Keller."

"Please, call me Art. We've known each other for several years, worked closely on those internship programs." He turned to her mom. "I refer to your daughter as my character witness. Let me escort you to the bar and get you a drink."

Her mom put a hand on his arm. "It would be a pleasure."

He chuckled with visible relief and led her away. Her mom threw a laughing glance back at Leanne, who waved, a trifle bemused. Her mom with Art Keller? She wondered who would charm the other first.

It felt weird seeing her mom with a man, even if only to get a drink at a party. Her conversation with Mark several weeks before echoed in her mind. Her mom had never dated or paid any attention to men, even after Leanne had grown and moved to her own apartment. Why now?

The answer washed over her like a spring rainstorm, sudden, cold and unexpected. Lionel was dead.

How that changed things for her mom, she'd have to ask. Maybe her mother felt free now. Had she wanted him to come for her, maybe expected it after his wife died? Had she been hurt when he hadn't? Thoughts similar to these tortured Leanne. How could she not have noticed her mom hurting?

"Hi," Mark said at her side.

Leanne jumped, sloshing her water. She held the glass away from her dress. "Oh, hi. Didn't see you."

"You were lost in thought, and not pleasant thought by the scowl on your face."

"What?"

"People have been avoiding coming near. Your frown scared them all off." He rocked on his heels. "I braved your displeasure, however, because I'm made of sterner stuff."

"A real he-man, huh?"

"Absolutely." He sipped from his tumbler. "Anything I can do to help?"

"Help?"

"With your problem. Whatever it is making you scowl."

She smiled. "No problem, just some thoughts that are years late in coming."

His brow wrinkled.

She waved it away. "Never mind. So… You came."

"After such a gracious invitation, how could I refuse?"

She felt herself blush, remembering the way she'd thrown the invitation at him. "Yeah, well… Sorry about that."

"Really? You seemed to enjoy it at the time."

"It was a good moment," she said with a smile.

"For you." He dipped his head. "Quite the coup, getting Keller here. He is here, I take it?" Mark scanned the crowd.

She spotted her mother and Art walking together toward a less-occupied corner. "Yes, somewhere."

Mark caught her eye. "I'll have to make sure I say hello."

"You do that," she replied softly.

"Good connections are important in business."

Heat shivered across her skin at his tone and his intent gaze. She swallowed.

"Good connections," he continued, "are important in all aspects of life." He brushed the back of the fingers holding his tumbler across the back of hers. She gripped her water goblet.

"I agree." Her voice barely registered in the noise-filled room. The darkening of his eyes told her he'd heard.

"We should work on ours," he said. "See if we can't come to some…" His voice dropped. "Compromise."

No word had ever sounded so seductive.

He leaned toward her, and his breath brushed her lips. She stretched up to meet him. Only millimeters kept their mouths apart.

"I can't, not here," she whispered.

"When?" He ran the fingertips of his empty hand over her arm, across her shoulder, up the back of her neck.

She closed her eyes for a moment, aroused by his touch. Wanting more. "My place, after."

"Do you have any idea how much I want to kiss you?"

His husky voice scraped her nerve endings to life. She shivered, yearning for the same thing. "As much as I want you to, I hope."

"More than that, I'm sure. I can hardly think, hardly walk—" He smiled ruefully. "Thinking about us together."

"I'd say I'm sorry, but I'd be lying. I dream about us together, too."

His hand fell away and he straightened. So did she. The spell had broken. What had she been thinking? Why did he pull away? Had her confession been too bold?

"Art," Mark said, looking over her shoulder.

Leanne pivoted to see her mom and Art, the latter now shaking hands with Mark. She felt the heat increase in her face. Had they seen her coming on to Mark?

She met her mom's gaze, widened her eyes in question, and received the same look. Her mother turned to Mark and held out her hands. "Mark."

He took them, and she leaned forward to kiss his cheek.

"Jenny," Mark said. "You look beautiful."

She laughed. "I'm sure you say that to all the girls."

Not all of us. Leanne tipped her glass and finished the droplets remaining. An excuse to escape, she thought.

But she dare not leave Mark with Art Keller.

Fingers digging into her forearm distracted her, as her mother pulled her a step away from the men. "He asked me out," her mom hissed.

"What? Who?"

"Who do you think? Art. For God's sake, Leanne, what am I supposed to do?"

She shook her head. "I don't know, Mom. What do you want to do?"

"How should I know? I just met him."

"Do you want to get to know him better?"

"That's not the point."

"I'll take that as a yes," Leanne said.

Her mother narrowed her eyes at her. "Don't be cute.

He's very handsome, very nice, very charming. He likes the same books and movies I do. From the little we talked, we have a lot in common."

"Yeah, I see your problem."

"This is not funny," her mom whispered fiercely. "He's important to you. To the Collins thing."

Leanne went cold. "Oh, Mom. Don't date him because of that. Or not date him because of it."

"I can't just forget it. It's a factor."

"Why?" Leanne realized how their tête-à-tête must look and plastered on a smile. She dipped her head to acknowledge someone across the room—not that she saw anyone over there. Her pretense would keep people thinking everything was normal.

While her mother spun her in circles.

"Why?" her mom echoed. "If we don't get along, he may not meet with you. Then Mark wins the company, and it's all my fault."

"I doubt if that's how Art does business."

"How do I know for sure?"

Leanne took a deep breath. "Go out with him. Seriously, Mom, he's a nice guy. He may not deal with me or Mark, anyway, because of his past with Lionel."

"What if we do get along?" her mom asked breathlessly.

Ah, Leanne thought. "That'd be scary, huh?"

Her mom nodded. "Lee, I haven't dated since Lionel."

"Then you're long overdue." She wrapped an arm around her mom's shoulders and hugged her close. "My future doesn't depend on your dating or not dating Art Keller. Okay?"

She nodded.

"If you want to, do it. If you don't, don't."

Her mom glanced at Art. "He does remind me of an older Brad Pitt."

Leanne smiled. "I was thinking Robert Redford."

Her mom's eyes lit. "That works for me, too."

They laughed and rejoined the men.

"Now we can drop the business talk and enjoy the party," Art said. "Nothing like a beautiful woman to brighten a room, eh, Collins?"

Her mom blushed at the intensity in Art's eyes.

"Nothing at all, sir," Mark agreed.

Leanne didn't glance his way. *Too late, bud*, she thought. She didn't want a compliment forced out of him. If that even was a compliment for her. He could learn a thing or two about charm from Art.

She wondered what business they had been discussing. She peeked at Mark, unable to tell anything from his expression. Had he made headway?

"This party is a very good idea," Mark said. "Gets your graduates face time with the upper echelon. I'm honored you invited me."

"Is this your first party?" Art asked.

Leanne exchanged a glance with Mark. He stared back in a definite challenge.

"I'm sure you understand," she said to Art, "my former aversion to the Collins Company."

Art smiled. "But I hear you're not so averse to it now."

"Not quite as much."

"Well, hello, all." Harvey Croppey edged into their circle. He shook hands with each, almost drooling as

Leanne introduced him to her mother. "Very pleased to meet *you*."

Leanne braced herself, noticing that both other men had straightened and taken a closer stand by her mom.

"So you're her mother," Croppey said. "From what I've heard, Leanne here is Lionel's daughter."

Mark's jaw clenched. Art's hands fisted.

Her mom nodded an acknowledgment. "She is. Lionel and I had an illicit affair."

"Oh, uh…" Croppey's face turned red. He opened and closed his mouth. "So," he said to Leanne, "I heard you're going to take over the king of takeovers here." He gestured to Mark.

She leaned toward him and whispered, "I'm Lionel's bastard, out to take all he had."

Croppey took the napkin from under his glass and wiped his forehead. He darted a gaze from Leanne's smirk to her mother's wide-eyed innocence to Mark and Art's clenched hostility. "Well, okay. Got to talk to some people over there."

He all but ran.

"That wasn't kind," her mom scolded her, trying unsuccessfully to hide her smile.

"But it was fun," she said.

"I can't believe you said that," Mark said, shaking his head. He retrieved his own handkerchief and wiped off his right hand. Leanne noticed Art doing the same thing. "He'll spread it to anyone who'll listen. I know you were tempted, Leanne, but maybe that wasn't the wisest move."

"Maybe not," she conceded, watching as Croppey moved into a group of her students. After a moment, they laughed and looked around until spying her. They waved.

Thanks, guys, I needed that. "My students know better. They won't let him get away with it."

"She was protecting Jenny," Art said. "Can't blame her for that."

He took Jenny's hand. "Don't worry," he said, gazing into her face. "I won't let that gossip hound spread rumors about your daughter. Or you."

Her mom beamed. "Why, thank you, Art."

Mark turned to Leanne. "Did I miss something?"

She grinned. "Got to get here on time, bucko."

"So I noticed."

"Excuse me." A tall, slender redhead stepped in between Mark and Leanne. "It seems I'm a little late myself."

"Oh, Julia," Mark said. "You've been a while."

Mark glanced at Leanne, who narrowed her eyes.

Dammit. He couldn't believe he'd done something this stupid. He'd invited Julia as a buffer, hoping she'd distract him from Leanne. And partly for spite, he had to admit.

Now he just wanted her gone. He was a selfish bastard. Er, a son of a bitch, he amended.

"I got waylaid by an acquaintance," Julia said. "Otherwise, I'd have returned to your side from the powder room much sooner."

"I don't believe we've met." Leanne extended her hand.

Mark flushed, brought to account for failing to introduce Julia to the others. He wondered if Leanne had a palm-sized weapon concealed in her grip.

"I'm Leanne Fairbanks, your hostess."

Ouch. Even he felt her claws.

"Julia Simpson," she replied with a sharp glance at Mark.

He stepped in and introduced her to the other two. "Julia is the assistant financial officer at Accessories, Inc."

The company Mark intended to buy. Leanne's gaze shot to his. He nodded slightly and her stiff posture eased. He'd just as much as admitted this wasn't personal, but a business date. The knowledge gave her an edge over him, but he conceded it happily. He didn't want her thinking he'd expressed interest in bedding her when he had an emotional tie to someone else.

"Mark and I have known each other for years," Julia said.

"How nice," Jenny said. "It's so comfortable to have an old friend to go places with."

Mark turned his chuckle into a cough. Leanne's lips quirked as she fought a smile. Art didn't bother; he just laughed.

Julia didn't.

Mark felt sorry for her. Mother and daughter defended their own.

Julia turned her back to the others. "I could use a drink, Mark. Let's go find the bar."

Mark glanced around the group, then shrugged. "Excuse us."

He felt Leanne's eyes boring into his back as he escorted Julia to the bar. So much for getting together at her place later.

Chapter Seven

"Mom," Leanne called as she unlocked her mother's front door. "It's me."

Leanne always knocked first. Her mom teased her, saying this had been Leanne's home, she certainly didn't need to knock. Leanne felt it gave her mom some privacy, ownership or whatever. After all, it was no longer Leanne's home.

"Mom," she called again, scanning the front room. Deep-pink roses sat on every surface and smelled divine. Three vases of long-stemmed blooms spread their rich fragrance through the room. She wandered into the kitchen. Two jelly jars containing cut-off blossoms brightened the counter. Why had her mom bought so many roses?

She heard movement upstairs and headed that way. Clothes lay strewn across almost every surface of her mom's bedroom, including the floor. Dresses, pantsuits and blouses decorated the queen-sized bed in a wilder pattern than the crazy quilt which adorned it. The nightstand held only a clock and a small vase of velvety pink roses. Her mom raked a hanger across the rail, saying something under her breath. Cursing, by the tone of it.

"What in the world is going on?" Leanne asked.

"Oh!" Her mom spun around, a hand over her chest. Wild blond hair stuck out every which way. Scarlet dusted her cheeks. "You scared me to death."

"I'm not surprised you couldn't hear me, with all the muttering you were doing. Are you having a yard sale?"

"Don't I wish." She groaned. "I'm getting ready for a date."

Leanne dropped onto the bed. "A date?"

Her mom glowered, then turned back to the closet, hands on her hips. "You've heard of them," she addressed the few remaining clothes on hangers. "A man and woman go out, have a horrible time, make fools of themselves and end the evening relieved it's over."

Leanne connected the dots. She nodded in approval at the flowers. Nice touch. "With Art?"

"Yes, with Art. Although why I agreed I'll never know."

This situation required humor or her mom would fuss herself into a frenzy. "He's charming, suave, rich and could probably melt off your underwear with his smile."

"Leanne!" Her mom whirled around, cheeks flaming.

"This room is a disaster, young lady," Leanne said. "Don't think you're going out tonight with it looking like this."

"Oh, you're hilarious, aren't you?"

"I try." Leanne stood and put clothes back on hangers. She evaluated the violet sundress in her hand. Such a thin material might be a little too cool. "Where are you going?"

"Dinner and a movie."

"Classic first date." Leanne considered the dress again. With a light sweater, it would be fine. Didn't she recall her mom having a gauzy wrap? She skimmed a glance over the chaos on the floor.

"We talked about movies at your party, so he knows I like them." Her mom reached for hangers and started in on the mess as well. "I should call and tell him I'm sick."

"Mom, don't. You'll be fine. It's just nerves."

"I know it's nerves, but they're making me sick." She put a hand to her stomach and closed her eyes.

Leanne frowned at her, assessing whether her suffering was a coincidence or stemmed from her evening out. The latter, she thought. Still, she moved aside the clothes on half of the bed and led her mom over. "Just lie down for a few minutes."

"I can't," her mom said, doing just that. "I have to find something to wear. Then I have to get dressed, go out and pretend I'm not going to throw up."

Leanne laughed. "It's just like my party. You didn't want to go, but once you got there, you had fun."

Her mom opened one eye. "This is all your fault."

"I know," Leanne said. "When you get home and you've had a wonderful time, remember then it was all my doing."

Her mom grunted. Leanne grinned. She set aside three selections and hung the rest. She put out shoes to coordinate with each outfit. "What time is he coming?"

"Oh." Her mom propped herself on an elbow, glancing at the clock. "An hour. I should get ready."

Leanne guided her through the process, recalling her own first attempts at dating as a teenager. Her mom had helped her in much the same way, although where her mom now stood quietly during the ministrations, Leanne had chattered.

The doorbell rang.

Her mom recoiled as though jabbed with a pin. Leanne clapped a hand to her own chest. They giggled. "Thank God I'd finished your mascara," Leanne said.

"You'd think we'd never seen a man before, let alone had one come to the house."

"You look great, Mom. I'll go let him in." Leanne turned and winked before she shut the bedroom door. "I need to give him The Talk."

"Leanne Colleen, don't you dare."

She chuckled to herself as she headed downstairs and opened the door. "Hi, Art."

"Oh, Leanne. I didn't expect you."

"Come on in." She glanced at his casual sports coat and slacks and decided the sundress had been a good choice.

"Jenny told me you had your own place," he said, walking into the small front room, glancing around. A smile touched his mouth, and Leanne figured he'd noticed the roses. Then he shot her a wide-eyed glance. "Not that it isn't nice to see you. Just that it's unexpected."

She found his nervousness endearing. "I have an apartment on Rush Street."

He raised his eyebrows. "You a party girl?"

She raised her eyebrows. "You a florist?"

He blushed, and they both laughed. "I went a little overboard, didn't I?"

"My mom loves them. It was a good move."

He sobered. "I didn't mean it as a 'move.' This isn't a chess game. I like your mother."

Leanne cocked her head. "I figured as much."

"I don't want you to think I'm taking advantage of her. She's a nice woman."

"I agree." How strange for him to lecture her on her mother's merits.

"Just because she was involved with Lionel Collins, don't think I don't respect her."

"Ah." Now it made sense. "Art, the way you defended my mom the other night when Croppey started in on her, I know you're not out to dishonor her." Jeez, had she walked down the stairs and into another century?

His expression cleared. "Good. I'm glad we got that straightened out."

"Me, too," Leanne said. Bizarre. Her mom was fifty-four, and Art somewhere in his early sixties. Yet here Leanne was, listening to Art's honorable intentions and okaying their date. She shook her head. People sure got crazy when they dated, no matter their age.

"So." Art shoved his hands in his pockets. "How're things at Collins?"

She tilted her hand from side to side. "So-so. I'm working on a project now that's getting trickier by the moment."

"Anything I can do to help?"

Leanne grinned at the irony. "I'll let you know. What movie are you two going to see?"

They talked of several new releases until her mom made her appearance. Which was the only way to regard it, Leanne thought. Her mom entering a room made one want to genuflect. She had a presence along with her natural beauty.

Art jerked to attention and forgot Leanne existed.

JENNY LAUGHED at Art's imitation of the movie theater ticket-taker. The teen had been full of his own importance. She'd anticipated a dreadful evening, full of awkward silences until they realized they had little in common. Art delighted her with small talk, keeping her too distracted for nerves. The movie had been action-packed, leaving her feeling as though she didn't meet the characters at all. Not bad for what it was, she thought. Just not her flavor of tea. Still, she'd suggested it, knowing the lead actor would be the talk of the hair salon for the next few months. It never hurt to be up on these things.

Art pushed open the door of Carson's, the restaurant he'd chosen. Known for its ribs, it also featured mouth-watering steaks and the best hamburgers Jenny had ever tasted. She hadn't wanted to go anywhere expensive, even though Art didn't have to watch his budget the way she did. He probably didn't even have a budget.

Still, Jenny had eaten there twice and felt secure in its choice. She worried they'd have to wait for a table, knowing the conversation would eventually center on her. They hadn't used up their luck for the evening. Only a few couples stood in the waiting area inside the door. She took a seat on the red vinyl-covered bench and endeavored to conjure up more polite conversation.

"Ten minutes," Art said, returning to her side. "That doesn't even count as a wait here."

She smiled, feeling the stretch of her mouth. What could they discuss that would fill the time?

He sat beside her and turned her way. "You know, Jenny, I'm having a wonderful time. Thank you."

"You are?"

"I don't date often. It's still awkward for me."

"It is?" Jenny mentally rolled her eyes. She sounded like a witless parrot.

"I'm not sure if you know, but my wife died three years ago. Cancer."

She put her hand on the back of his where it rested near his knee. "I didn't know. Art, I'm sorry."

"Thanks." He took a breath. "She didn't have much warning. We were barely over the shock of hearing the diagnosis when it all went to hell."

He rubbed his other hand down his face.

"How horrible for you."

"It was. Some days, it still is." He shook his head, seeming to return to the restaurant. "I got out of town, but traveling alone made it worse. So I threw myself into Kellco, but I just don't care about the company the same way now. Getting used to being alone has been a long process."

"I understand." She got his message. The date wasn't working for him, and he was letting her down gently. Blaming it on himself.

"Anyway," he said, "I don't find it easy trying to romance a woman. So if I mess up, cut me some slack, okay?"

She smiled. "You don't have to romance me. Let's just be friends, enjoy the evening out."

"No, that's not what I want, Jenny." He turned his hand palm up and held hers. "Let me try this again. I've been uncomfortable on previous dates. Not this one. Before, I've thought, why bother? But tonight it's different. With you."

Her mouth went dry. "I haven't dated since my relationship with Lionel."

He nodded, not breaking eye contact. "I wondered."

"Wondered if I make a habit of getting involved? Of having affairs with married men?"

"No, I wondered if you were involved with anyone. You don't seem to realize the effect you have on men. On me."

She gulped.

Just then, their table became available. Jenny stood, wishing she could decipher Art's thoughts. Her effect on him? What did he mean by that? So much for him not enjoying the date. She'd lost what little ability she'd once had figuring out the male species.

The maître d' led them to a table along the wall away from the bustle of the room. She hid behind her menu, not seeing the words, until Art touched her hand. Held on to it.

"I shouldn't have said all that, not so soon. Let's see what happens, okay?" He squeezed her hand. "I just wanted you to know if I seem ill at ease, it's because of my long dry spell. Not because of you."

"*Your* long dry spell?"

He chuckled. "Well, I guess you win that one."

"So," Jenny ventured, "if I seem tongue-tied, it's because I haven't done more than flirt with a man in thirty years."

"I have to ask, and I hope this doesn't upset you. Are you in mourning for him?"

She sighed. "Yes and no. I did my grieving years ago, but he did just die, so memories surface sometimes. However, if you're asking if I'm still in love with him, the answer is no. I got over Lionel when I had Leanne. I put him away like out-of-fashion shoes."

Art barked out a laugh.

"Maybe that sounds heartless. Nevertheless, I had to move on. I'll always love Lionel for giving me Leanne, but that's all I've felt for some time now."

"Then why haven't you dated?"

"I didn't meet a man I wanted to spend time with." She glanced away, face burning. *Let the floor just open up and swallow me.* Had she just admitted that out loud? Practically thrown herself at him?

His hand tightened on hers. "I like that answer."

"Please, pretend you didn't hear it."

He snorted. "Not likely. I'm glad. Maybe now that we've cleared the air, admitted our nerves and our attraction, we can be comfortable with each other."

She took her hand back, sipped her water. "That's a little harder for me because of Leanne."

"Leanne?"

"Your relationship with her."

Art blinked. "My…? We've worked together on the intern program the university. That's it."

"I know. I meant now. The Collins thing."

"You've lost me."

Jenny cocked her head, debating. If Leanne hadn't mentioned it, she had good reason. She probably wouldn't want her mother interfering in a business matter. On the other hand, it never hurt to have a connection. Networking, Jenny thought it was called.

She took a breath. "Leanne hasn't told you, I guess, and probably doesn't want me to. But Lionel's will put her in competition against Mark. The winner gets CoCo."

He sat silent. She could almost see the wheels and cogs in his brain processing data. Rich and smart. What did he see in her?

"Okay," Art said. "I'd heard rumors of something along those lines. What does it have to do with me?"

MARK KNOCKED on Leanne's door Saturday afternoon. She'd buzzed him into the building, puzzlement clear in her voice even over the intercom. He should have called but feared she would put him off. He couldn't have this discussion at work.

She opened the door wearing what he considered her usual at-home clothes, jeans and a T-shirt. This one, navy blue and from the Shedd Aquarium, depicted a beluga whale popping out of the water, its white mouth open in a dolphin-like smile.

"What do you want?" she asked.

And showing its teeth.

He pushed past her into her apartment. The door shut behind him with force. He shoved his hands in his pockets and turned to face her. "Put on some shoes. I want to talk to you, and I can't do it here."

"Don't tell me what to do. And what's wrong with my apartment? That is, if I were going to talk to you, which seems unlikely at the rate you're going."

Mark stepped closer, invading her space. He liked the way her eyes widened with awareness of him. He liked the way she didn't back down. He liked the way she smelled when he got this close, all feminine and warm. He liked every damned thing about her, which was why they couldn't stay here.

"I'm not trying to bully you," he said quietly. "Please put on some shoes. I can't talk to you here because we're alone, and I can't stop thinking there must be a bedroom down the hall."

She gasped. "And that concerns you, how?"

He took hold of her upper arms. "You know how. At

your function the other evening, we made a date to return here. To your apartment," he emphasized. "We're attracted to one another, Leanne. Don't pretend you don't know what I'm talking about."

"Our 'date' the other evening was interrupted by the woman you brought to the party."

Mark gave her a gentle shake. "A business date. I told you that."

She turned her head away. He curled a finger under her chin and brought her gaze back to his. A faint pink tinged her cheeks.

"I want to get to know you. I think you want the same thing. If I'm wrong, tell me now."

"You're not wrong," she whispered.

"Good. Then let's go for a drive or a quiet drink. Somewhere we can talk."

Leanne nodded and went down the hall. Mark blew out the breath he'd been holding, unaware of his tension until it lessened. She'd admitted being attracted to him. He could scratch one worry from his list.

He prowled the room, still too anxious to sit. He studied the framed photographs she displayed, most of her mom with some touristy sign as a backdrop. Beaches and woods appeared occasionally. He peered at a younger Leanne dangling a catfish from a fishing pole, a horrified expression on her face. He laughed.

"That's my reminder," she said, coming into the room, "never to go fishing again."

He turned to her. "Where was this taken?"

"Michigan. My mom decided I needed some outdoorsy experiences when I was little. Get me away from the city."

She shuddered. "After too many bugs, camping got crossed off the list. Fortunately, she'd only borrowed camping gear from a friend at the salon, not bought it.

"The fish, however, was the final straw. We dragged it through the water, keeping it breathing, until we found this nice man who took it off the hook. After that, we stayed strictly away from nature. To this day, neither of us can eat catfish."

Mark laughed and set down the picture. "I would have figured you for the outdoors type."

"Why?" She eyed him. "You like that kind of thing?"

He shuddered as she had a moment earlier, making her laugh. "A walk in Lincoln Park is enough nature for me. However, I do like the zoo."

"Animals in cages suit me fine."

She walked to the door. He touched her arm, keeping her from unlocking it.

"Just one thing first," he said.

When he drew her into his arms, she came willingly, settling her body against his. He bit back a groan, liking the way her breasts nestled against him, then leaned down and kissed her.

The softness of her lips made him hard. He wrapped her closer, inhaling her scent, robbing them both of breath. She tasted of mint toothpaste, making him want to smile while at the same time desiring her even more.

He pulled back while he could. His control felt shaky at best. As much as he wanted to make love to her, he wanted to get to know her even more. Well, almost as much.

They left her building and drove in silence. Mark

enjoyed the peace and planned what he'd say once they arrived. She'd admitted being attracted to him, but he needed a lot more than that for what he had in mind. Would she be open to his suggestion? Did the connection he'd felt at the party have a chance to develop? With their rocky start behind them, their relationship could only get easier.

"Where are we going?" Leanne asked.

"Lake Geneva."

"Wisconsin?"

He laughed at the incredulous tone in her voice. "I thought we'd walk along the beach. It'll be quiet and away from everything." He shot her a smile. "Not too outdoorsy for you, is it?"

"No, but it's kind of far. We have a lake in our own city, Mark, bigger than Geneva. You've heard of Lake Michigan, I take it? It has a beach."

"With skyscrapers two blocks away." He shook his head. "I want to escape that for a while. Lake Geneva's only about a hundred miles north, just over the state border."

She didn't object, just dug in her purse for a few minutes. Then she adjusted the air vents. Three times.

He smiled to himself. "Why don't you find us some music? It's satellite radio, so you should be able to find something to your taste."

"What do you like?"

"Anything but country or rap."

"Amen." She grinned at him and began fiddling with the radio.

"Or gospel," he added.

She laughed, and he relaxed.

The drive took only an hour and a half, in spite of construction work along the interstate. He parked in a public parking lot and stretched after locking the car.

"Smell that fresh air," she said, gazing out to the lake. Trees lined the opposite side, far in the distance. This side of the shore boasted a short rocky beach between boat docks.

He noticed the gleam in her eyes and took her remark as teasing. "Don't worry, we're not staying long enough for it to clean the pollution out of your lungs."

She chuckled and walked beside him. "Pretty."

Clear blue water reflected the few white clouds overhead. A slight, chilly breeze blew strands of her hair across her cheek. Mark ached to trace it away, feel her skin under his fingers, watch her skin flush pinker with awareness of him. Was it too early for such intimacy?

"This used to be a glacier. That's why the water is such a deep blue." He took her hand.

Her gaze darted to his. He held it, then saw the tension fall from her shoulders, felt her fingers curl around his.

"Tell me about growing up being best friends with your mom," he said, considering it a safe introduction to their life stories. What better way to get to know one another?

They strolled toward the water.

"It was great. Although we were close, she was still in charge. We weren't equals, but being friends helped us through some of the hard times."

"What hard times?"

Leanne shrugged. "Lack of money. Eating scrambled eggs for dinner and bologna for lunch because she was saving to buy the salon where she worked. My teenage hormones."

"I thought the Lion sent money."

"She never touched it. Not after she got back on her feet from having me, anyway. I had a playpen in the shop, then later a designated area for schoolwork and a TV."

"No nanny." What would it have been like, he wondered, to spend so much time with one's mother? He couldn't imagine tagging along with Gloria to her many charity meetings, bridge parties or lunches with her friends. Thank God. The very idea made him queasy.

"No, no nanny. No babysitter. She could have put in another chair and afforded a sitter for me, but she didn't."

"Another chair?"

"A station for another hairdresser."

He nodded.

"As owner, she gets paid by the other hairdressers in her salon. But she wanted me with her. She had a window put in over my corner and had a fan blow all the chemicals away from me. I remember she always had the doctor checking me when I was small."

She pointed to a small orange sailboat. "Hey, look at that kid. He can't be more than eight. He's going to tip over!"

They watched the craft tilt, then the boy surfaced with a laugh. His antics while trying to turn his boat over made them smile. When he got it upright, they cheered along with several boaters who'd stopped near the boy, ready to lend a hand if needed.

"Look like fun?" Mark asked.

"No."

He chuckled. "I didn't think so, either. Give me a nice, slow pontoon boat with a reliable motor."

"Give me a nice chair on a restaurant patio to watch you from."

"That sounds good, too."

"How was your date with Julia?" Leanne asked when they continued walking.

He squeezed her hand in reassurance. "All business."

"Did you convince her to sell you Accessories?"

"I've got a meeting with their board."

"Mark, that's wonderful." Her beaming smile felt warmer than the Wisconsin sun.

"It was your idea and your research. If you still want in, that's fine by me."

She shook her head. "I don't think Julia would be too happy to see me as part of your team."

His gut tightened. Part of his team. It sounded good to him. They discussed the particulars of the buyout, Leanne's comprehension of the details dead-on due to her research.

They stopped to watch boats easing in and out of the marina. After ten minutes or so had passed, they decided on an early dinner.

They debated the lure of the quaint little town's offerings and decided, not too surprisingly, on fish. "We missed the fish boil last night," Mark noted on one sign.

"Eew. Thank goodness."

He laughed, falling under her spell. Her humor was just one more thing he'd discovered he liked about her. "Not feeling adventurous?"

She made a disgusted face. "Not that adventurous. I'll take my fish one identifiable piece at a time."

Deciding against the well-known resort, they located an "adorable" house, according to Leanne, which had been turned into a restaurant serving only dinner. The hostess in the foyer led them into the former parlor of the house, now outfitted with ten small tables for four. Burgundy tablecloths lent warmth to each area, while fat gray candles burned in glass holders. Once seated, Mark opted to drink water as he had the long drive back to negotiate, and Leanne did the same.

She leaned toward him and pointed to her menu, then whispered, "Does this fish come with a face?"

He burst out laughing, and she swatted his arm. Her complexion glowed hotly. "Shhh."

He double-checked where she indicated and wished she'd pointed out trout or something more exotic than white-fish.

"You can order yours without a face," he said, holding in his amusement. "As a matter of fact, I dare you."

So, of course, she did. The waiter's lips twitched, but he solemnly assured her the food would not have a personality.

Mark shook his head. Leave it to Leanne to charm the locals.

"What was growing up like for you?" Leanne asked as she tore open her crusty bread.

Mark shrugged. "Nice house. No bologna or eggs for dinner, but we had struggles."

"Such as?"

"I don't know. Not money trouble, but there was…a coldness—" He shook his head, the description not quite accurate. "A gulf between my parents and me. Warren worked all the time. Gloria helped out with her side of the business, hostessing and all that. We didn't spend the time together that you and Jenny did."

"I doubt if most kids do. Our relationship is pretty unique. My friends don't understand it now, let alone when I was younger." Leanne pursed her lips.

Mark swallowed the urge to lean over and kiss her.

"So who did you spend time with?" she asked.

"Oh." He cleared his throat. "Nannies, when I was little. Friends at boarding school."

"Boarding school?"

The horror in her tone made him smile. "I liked it. The atmosphere was so different from home." He shook his head, remembering. The two addresses were miles apart, not just in distance, but also in the fun he experienced in each. Strange that the strict boarding school had allowed him more freedom than home.

"All those boys," he said. "We got into some trouble. Not enough that our parents had to be notified, mind you, but enough to build friendships."

"Your childhood pals are all hooligans?"

He laughed. "Now they're respected businessmen and lawyers. So, yeah, some are still flirting with the law."

Leanne smiled. "Your parents would have disapproved of your antics?"

"Our parents would have killed us for disgracing our family names. That's why we made sure to keep our adventures just under the radar."

"Sounds pretty good having buddies like them."

"We were a tight group." He frowned as he realized he hadn't kept in touch with any of them.

They talked about their friends, past and present, and told stories of childhood antics. When the food came, he regretted the interruption and hoped, by her slight frown, that she did as well.

The waiter, a man in his forties who certainly knew how to work the customers, presented her plate with a flourish. "I hope this satisfies the lady."

"No face?" Mark teased her about the fish.

"It's lovely," she told the waiter. He bowed and left them with a quiet chuckle.

Leanne smiled around her forkful of whitefish. After swallowing, she said, "If it melted in my mouth like this, I almost wouldn't care if it stared at me the whole time."

They discussed people at work, but only in terms of personalities and recent amusing tales, and didn't delve into business talk.

With reluctance, Mark signaled for the check.

"Madam found everything to her liking?" the waiter asked with comical formality and a twinkle in his eye.

Leanne smiled. "I hardly knew what I was eating."

"Your compliment shall be relayed to the chef," he said.

They walked back to the car hand in hand, now almost feeling comfortable with it. Twilight turned the sky gray.

"I can't believe," Leanne said as they detoured to the lake again, "how different our parents were, yet we have so much in common."

He hesitated, not certain how to phrase what he needed to say. The example to best illustrate his feelings might sound absurd. "Your mom's a toucher. I noticed the other night."

"Yeah?" She said it as a question, waiting for the connection.

He dreaded telling the story but didn't know if he could

make it clear any other way. The explanation he'd come up with would have to do. "I used to have this dream, until I was around five."

She nodded encouragingly.

"I'm little, a baby probably. I wake up and it's dark. I'm crying, waiting for someone to come. To hold me, cover me up, sing to me, whatever." He shrugged, unsure what that baby cried out for. "No one comes."

Leanne stopped walking.

"Gloria says it's a memory from my first two years, when I lived in the orphanage. But that waiting feeling never went away. The nightmares did, but wanting someone to come... When I think back on my childhood, I think of those dreams."

"Wow."

"Yeah." He threw a pebble into the lake. "Pretty screwed up, huh?"

"No. Just sad."

"I don't want your pity. I just wanted you to understand why I envy you. What you had with your mom, even without money—which you two could have had, if Jenny had cashed those checks—it's a better life than you might think."

"Oh, Mark, you're wrong. I totally appreciate what I've got. Money never meant anything to my mom, so it isn't a big priority for me, either."

He took her hand and continued walking. "What is important to you?"

"The usual things." She shrugged. "Happiness, love, a family someday. The respect of my colleagues. My teaching."

"Family. That's something I want, too. Soon."

"I know. I'm thirty. I hear that clock ticking."

"I'm thirty-four," he said. "Not the same biological thing, but I'm tired of my empty apartment."

Lonely, he could have said, but how pathetic was that? He still couldn't believe he'd told her about his childhood nightmares. Sheesh.

Leanne walked along with Mark, holding hands. What a change today had brought. Now she could envision them dating, could see it going further. Marriage? Way too soon even to think about, but the idea appealed to her.

Funny all the things they had in common. She loved his sense of humor, his easy manner. Being quiet together in the car and along the lake felt natural, not strained as silence had been with other men. She didn't feel as though she had to entertain him or pander to his moods. She liked him.

More than liked him, if she was honest. She slid a glance his way, watching the breeze ruffle his hair.

Mark was breathtakingly handsome. She had no problem picturing them making love. She had more of a problem not thinking about it.

She wondered if his nightmare really had happened in the orphanage. Or had it happened after his adoption? She couldn't picture Gloria as the maternal type, and she had no idea what Warren had been like.

She wanted to ask. Warren was, after all, her half-brother. Something held her back. Fear, she guessed, to discover Warren had been just like Lionel. Not that it would come as a surprise, but she didn't want to believe Mark had been cast from the same mold. Surely someone in his family had a decent streak.

"I was thinking," Mark said slowly, "if we started dating, it might be awkward at work."

"Might be. Are we going to start dating?"

He glanced at her. "I'd like to."

"Me, too." She smiled at him, unable to hide her feelings.

He let go of her hand and put his arm around her waist. She burned with awareness, the heat of his body catching fire with hers. She slipped her arm behind his back, holding on to his shirt. Their hips bumped.

Leanne swallowed. His kiss earlier in her apartment had surprised her with its timing, but had felt natural, like the next step in their relationship. She wouldn't have objected if he'd led her down the hall to her bedroom. Or the living-room sofa. Or the floor where they'd stood.

"And you have your teaching," he said.

"What?" She blinked, coming back to the conversation. She lifted her face to the breeze and relished its chill brush against her heated skin.

"Your teaching. So you don't really have to work at Collins to be happy. You said that before. That teaching is one of the things that makes you happy."

She stopped, sure she'd misunderstood him. "You think I should quit Collins?"

His mouth opened and closed. She could see his effort to find words. "I think you might want to consider it."

She stepped away from him and started walking. "Let me think about it. Right now, I'm getting cold." Was she ever. She couldn't believe she'd fallen for his romancing her, just to get her to withdraw from the competition. "Can you take me home?"

"Sure." He bent and peered into her face. "You okay?"

"Just a little wind-burnt and too much good food."

They didn't say much on the ride back.

"Tired," she answered when he asked what was wrong.

"Just pull up in front of my building," she said. "You don't have to park."

"Leanne."

"I'll see you Monday at work, okay?" She smiled for him, hoping it appeared convincing.

"I'll call you tomorrow."

"Sure." She hopped out of the car. At the door, she forced herself to turn and wave. He drove off, the frown on his face unmistakable.

Once inside her apartment, she kicked off her shoes, and picked up the phone.

"Art? It's Leanne Fairbanks."

Chapter Eight

Leanne seated herself opposite Art Keller's desk on Monday afternoon, trying to appear composed while he signed some papers with his assistant, a thirtyish, pretty brunette with perky efficiency. Mark had inherited seventy-two-year-old Mrs. Pickett, and, to his credit, hadn't replaced her. Maybe because he was single, he had to be more cautious. Art had been in love with his wife and still mourned her. Or had until he met Leanne's mother.

To accomplish the second task in Lionel's will, she had to convince Art to take a meeting with the Collins people and discuss the buyout of his company. If he agreed, it would be because of her, since he wouldn't meet with Mark. She wondered if Art would have agreed to a meeting before his interest in her mother. Now they'd started dating, she felt she was exploiting a friend.

Damn Mark Collins for putting her in this position. She had to win, to show him where he could put his manipulation tactics. He was no different than Lionel, and the realization broke her heart.

How dare Mark suggest she quit Collins and drop out

of the competition? The nerve of the man still enraged her. It galled her that she'd fallen for his act. Welcomed it. Returned his affection, but with sincerity on her part.

"I'm glad you called, Leanne," Art said when his assistant closed the door behind her. "I'd been thinking quite a bit about you."

"Oh?"

"About my agreement to consider dealing with you as regards Collins Company's buying out Kellco."

"I hope you've had positive thoughts." She wiped her palms on her skirt, trying to be inconspicuous.

"I want to be upfront with you." He fiddled with a pen for a moment before meeting her eyes. "Jenny told me about the situation Lionel's will put you in."

She swallowed, sure her face flamed. "I didn't ask my mother to pave the way for me."

He nodded. "She said you would be upset with her. Please don't be. Knowing about the competition has given me time to consider my options."

"I gathered from your comment the other day at the restaurant—that you'd heard I was organizing a coup—that rumors had circulated. I would have told you the specifics, Art. I don't want you to think I schemed behind your back."

He smiled. "You mean you didn't bring your mother to the UIC party to distract me?"

She shook her head.

"Well, it worked, anyway." He sat forward. "But I'm not a pathetic old coot whose head is easily turned by an attractive woman. I don't do business with that part of my anatomy."

"I never thought you did," Leanne whispered. *Kill me now*. She'd never suffered such mortification. She definitely didn't want to think about Art's anatomy, especially in relation to her mother.

"Glad we understand each other. Any consideration I give you will be based on our past relationship through the intern programs. As much as I care about Jenny, I wouldn't sell my company to her daughter just to…gain favors."

Leanne nodded, unable to speak, wishing he wouldn't use words like *anatomy* or *favors*. The pictures they conjured tested her embarrassment level.

Tested her?

She regarded Art and decided he was a sly negotiator himself. Squaring her shoulders, she mentally crossed her fingers. *Please let me be right.*

"I understand what you're saying, Mr. Keller. Let me assure you, I don't want my mother to be a factor in these negotiations. Should the Collins Company agree to purchase Kellco," as though this were his idea, she thought, "I need you to understand I couldn't misrepresent the acquisition price just because you're a…" She deliberately paused. "Family friend."

His eyebrow arched. She returned his stare.

Silence ticked in the room. Leanne waited for the explosion.

"I would deal exclusively with you," Art said, "not Mark Collins. That's a deal-breaker."

She let her breath out slowly. Held in her glee.

"I understand."

He nodded. "I'll consider an offer then."

She stood and leaned over his desk, extending her hand.

If he noticed she had to brace herself, perhaps he'd credit it to her lack of height, not her unsteady legs.

Art came around the desk to walk her out. At the door, he paused. "Gutsy move."

She grinned, then swallowed it quickly.

"I like the confidence, Leanne. It looks good on you."

"Thanks." She couldn't contain her smile. High praise from a master, she thought.

"Off the record?" he said.

"Sure."

"I had a good time with your mom. I'm sorry for insinuating your mother and I might be intimate. I just wanted to make it clear that has no part in our dealings."

"Believe me, I wasn't going mention it."

He laughed. "It had to be said. Hope I didn't embarrass you too much."

"Let's just forget it. What happens between you two stays between you two."

"Deal." He shook her hand, patted it with his left.

She hailed a taxi to go back to the university, trying to dismiss the daughterly feelings Art engendered.

LEANNE KEPT the news to herself for two days. When the judging panel reconvened Wednesday afternoon, she entered the boardroom feeling smug.

She'd show that insufferable Mark Collins a thing or two about manipulation.

In the past few days, her voice-mailbox had filled with his attempts to reach her. She'd e-mailed him at work, blaming her absence at Collins on her duties at school, keeping the tone professional. Finals, interviews. Any excuse she could make up. He'd had the sense not to come to her apartment. His calls had stopped on Tuesday. Leanne didn't know whether he'd lost interest or just counted on seeing her in the boardroom.

Mark arrived ahead of her. He didn't turn when she entered, although his posture stiffened as though he sensed her presence. She pulled out the upholstered armchair next to his and sat.

When he didn't speak, didn't turn toward her, didn't try to initiate contact of any kind, her nerves frayed. She darted a glance his way. He was studying some papers in front of him, or appeared to be, anyway.

Ignoring her? Leanne shut off her indignation. The pretense of closeness in Wisconsin had been a trick to make her pull out of the competition. She wondered if he still thought she would. Did he think he had Collins in the bag? Was that why he didn't feel a need to charm her now? Did he feel that secure?

She put away her bruised ego and suppressed the voice saying the pain went deeper than that. She didn't long for him. If last weekend she'd become a little infatuated... Well, she hadn't, so it didn't matter.

The three panel members filed into the room, once again garbed in dark colors. Today the apparel seemed appropriate. She was going to bury Mark Collins.

His clean scent of man and soap wafted in her direction. Leanne turned her head away, not immune to his attractiveness. Sure, he looked scrumptious and smelled nice. So did fudge, an abundance of which added inches she didn't need. She could resist temptation. Especially since she'd had a taste of his true flavor and found it bitter.

Harrison Mulvany stood. His silver hair gleamed in the brightly lit room. The matching glint in his eye said he planned to enjoy this. "I'm sure you're both anxious regarding today's meeting. As you'll recall, this committee is well aware of the futility of approaching Kellco to discuss acquiring it."

He gestured to the members on either side of him. They nodded. "We have agreed," he said, "to stand by the intent of Lionel Collins's will, which was to have one of you win the second task. Therefore, we'll listen to a report of your efforts and choose from those. The steps you took will have more weight than the progress you regrettably couldn't make."

Leanne maintained a bland expression. They certainly assumed a lot based on past performances. Lionel and Mark had repeatedly failed. The panel had discounted her efforts before she'd even presented them. She didn't appreciate being overlooked or made to feel invisible and incapable. Their attitude would make her success sweeter.

"After hearing your efforts," he continued, "we will then listen to your strategy for a hostile takeover of Kellco."

Leanne gasped.

"This was Lionel's intent also," Mulvany said. "We have debated the issue during the past weeks with Mr. Collins's executor, Todd Benton, and feel this would honor the Lion's memory and best serve the Collins Company."

Leanne simmered. A hostile takeover would best serve Lionel's memory? What did that say about him? How could they do this to Art? They sat there calmly, plotting to steal the business he'd spent a lifetime building. A company into which he'd invested an abundance of love and honest hard work.

This was the essence of CoCo? This was what she was contending for? To head this company, to be a part of these kinds of maneuvers?

"Mark, I believe Ms. Fairbanks went first last time."

Mulvany sat, and Mark rose to his feet.

"As you've anticipated the outcome of the task," Mark said, "my report will come as no surprise in that area. I regret fulfilling those expectations."

You mean you struck out. His formality amused her. Couched in such careful terms, he didn't have to acknowledge his failure. He'd met the panel's expectations.

He couldn't admit failure because he still sought to earn his family name. She tried to ignore the twinges of sympathy and guilt the realization generated. This was business, she told herself. Mark certainly wouldn't let sentiment sway him. She remembered the feel of his arm around her waist as they'd walked around Lake Geneva. He'd used her feelings against her.

Resolve hardened, she listened as he outlined his attempts to reach Art Keller. He'd been tenacious in chasing his quarry, using phone, e-mail and personal contact. Yet he'd made no headway. She swallowed a smirk.

"I feel a measure of success," he said, "in the improved personal nature of my relationship with Mr. Keller. Although our talks did not lead to a formal meeting with his people, and granted, he wouldn't discuss a buyout with me, we do now have a friendly acquaintance. This had not been the case previously, nor had the Lion made any inroads in this manner."

He sat, adjusted his suit jacket, and turned to face her. His expression as featureless as a mannequin, one would think they'd never met. Never kissed. Never discussed a future.

It hurt.

She met his gaze, encountered a deep-brown abyss. Whatever he felt, he'd masked it behind indifference. Or he truly felt nothing for her.

Leanne stood, pushed in her chair and put on her game face. "As you've anticipated the outcome of the task," she repeated the first part of Mark's opening, "my report may come as a surprise."

The panel snapped to attention. Mark straightened more slowly, but she felt his stare burn into her.

"In short," she said, staring over the top of Mr. Garland's head, "I have secured Mr. Keller's promise to meet with a team from Collins." She slapped a manila folder on the black conference table. "These are the dates Kellco can meet with us. I've included a list of essential people from each relevant department to staff my team."

She heard a strangled gasp but didn't know whose.

"Yes, *my* team. Mr. Keller will not discuss a buyout of his company with Mr. Collins." She half turned toward Mark and met his now-hot gaze. "That's a deal-breaker."

Leanne raised an eyebrow at him, as though he could possibly question her. She'd proceeded without consideration for his feelings. He tightened his lips, but said nothing.

She returned her attention to the panel, who now sat with hands clasped on the tabletop, near-smiles on their faces. She had garnered their interest and possibly earned their respect. She couldn't care less.

She named the players she wanted beside her in this matter. It wasn't a necessary component to the challenge, which she'd undoubtedly won, and she'd have to present the same material to the entire board officially. However, the more she showed these representatives, the more she shoved her capability down their throats and Mark's. She might not have experience in the business arena, but she wasn't a witless ingénue. Perhaps now they would stop treating her as one.

She resumed her seat.

Mulvany smiled. "We must discuss this rather surprising turn of events. One moment please."

The panel didn't even rise. Mulvany bent his head toward Mrs. Metcalf while Mr. Garland leaned in.

Their whispers held no interest for Leanne. She knew she'd won. She wanted to hear them say it, to watch Mark squirm.

At least she'd saved Art from a hostile takeover. Still livid, she tried to set it aside. Hostile takeovers weren't unheard of. Firms purchased all available stocks of a company, then pursued their stockholders and paid them more than market value, thereby owning the majority. The idea just disturbed her because it was Art's company.

No, she had to be honest with herself. She didn't like this practice no matter whose company Collins acquired that way.

"Well," Mulvany said, wrenching her thoughts back, "our decision is fairly clear. Leanne, you have won this task and our admiration."

She inclined her head in acceptance of his compliment.

"We'll have to call you 'the young Lion,' Leanne. Oh!

Oh, I see. Lion, Leanne." Mulvany cleared his throat, red in the face.

Mark's scowl deepened.

"That makes the score, if you will, one task each." Mulvany frowned. "However, Mark, I don't see how you can compete any longer. The next task is, of course, to negotiate the purchase of Kellco. They won't meet with you. Do you wish to withdraw and concede the competition to Leanne?"

Mark rose to his feet, hands fisted at his sides. "No, I do not. Ms. Fairbanks has obtained a meeting. However, she has no authority to make this deal."

"As winner of this—" Mulvany started.

"But I don't recognize her as the winner," Mark growled. "I shall deal with Art Keller. He's agreed to meet with representatives of Collins. I am the head of Collins."

He stalked out of the room, leaving behind silence.

And a woman whose heart ached for him against her will. Leanne watched him go, knowing any possibility she'd had for a future with him left, too. It had been pretend, she admonished herself, eyes still on the door. *He didn't care for you. Wasn't falling in love with you.* She had to put away her foolish daydreams. He could never love her now. He'd never forgive her.

She shouldn't care after the way he'd used her. But she did. More than she'd realized.

Winning the task, winning the entire competition, meant nothing. She felt nothing. Except for the stabbing in her ribs, the hollowness of her chest, the burning of her throat, the sting of tears in her eyes.

"Congratulations, Ms. Fairbanks," Mrs. Metcalf said.

Recalled to the present, she shook hands with the panel members. Part of her future board of directors.

What had she done?

THAT NIGHT, Leanne took her problems to her mother. When she let herself in the house, she instinctively headed for the kitchen. The heavenly aroma of lasagna and garlic bread filled the air. Leanne put a hand to her stomach, not sure she could eat.

Now, if her mom had some nice wine, she'd be game. Heck, even bad wine would do the trick. Or vodka. Unfortunately, her mom didn't drink often enough to keep alcohol around.

"Hi, honey," her mom called over her shoulder as she rinsed a dish in the sink. "I'll just be a sec."

Leanne waited. Her mom turned and went still. Then she opened her arms. Leanne stepped into them, bathing her wounds with her mother's unconditional love. She didn't even have to speak. The comfort of her mother's embrace, the scent of Dove bar soap and a subtle lily-of-the-valley perfume signified home to her. Safety. Acceptance. Love.

"Oh, Mom, I screwed up."

Her mom rubbed her back, then kissed her cheek. She stepped away, still holding Leanne's hands. "Tell me."

"I betrayed Mark."

Her mother frowned. "I need details."

"And wine?" Leanne glanced at the table hopefully.

Her mom had laid out three place settings.

"None for you. I want a clear account of things. You can get sloshed afterward."

Leanne grimaced, knowing she wouldn't. She rarely drank, having no head for alcohol, either.

The third place setting disturbed her, bringing as it did memories of Mark at her apartment. The night he'd kissed her. The night he'd told her he couldn't have an affair with her while competing for Collins.

He'd been honest. Then, at least. All he'd mentioned was an affair, not forever.

Why the change of tactics in Wisconsin?

"Who's coming for dinner?" she asked.

"Art. Didn't I tell you?"

Leanne shook her head. She'd made a frantic, probably incoherent call to her mom, asking if she could come to dinner that evening. Of course, her mom had said yes.

"I can cancel," her mom said now.

"No." She swallowed her disappointment. "I'll come back tomorrow."

"You will not."

Leanne shot her a startled look, and they both laughed.

"I meant," her mom said, "you'll stay. You can come back tomorrow if you want. We'll be having leftovers."

Leanne inspected the salad, fresh green beans and single loaf of bread. "Been a while since you fed a man?"

"What do you mean?"

"The guys I've dated could eat all this by themselves."

Her mother's brow creased. "I don't have enough?"

"For tonight you do. Just don't expect leftovers."

"Hmm." Her mom turned and rummaged through the refrigerator. She pulled out a container of baby carrots and bags of celery and cauliflower. "Here, cut this up. I'll stir up some dip."

The simple chore gave Leanne time to fill her mom in on the basics. She left out the "date" in Wisconsin. "I won this phase, anyway."

"I'd say congratulations, but you're so unhappy."

"I had to call on Art." Her gaze sharpened. "By the way, don't do that again. This was business. If I'd wanted Art to know more, I'd have told him."

Her mom stared at her a moment in heavy silence, then said, "You're welcome."

Leanne flushed. "Sorry, I didn't mean to snap. But, Mom, it was humiliating to find out you'd told Art all about the conditions of Lionel's will."

"You know I only meant to help."

"I appreciate that, but I do all right by myself."

"That's what you said your first day of kindergarten."

Leanne laughed. "That's what I said the first day of kindergarten after you stood outside my room all day and peeked in the window."

"I wasn't the only mother out there." She handed Leanne a platter. "Spread those out pretty."

Leanne made a face. "Not my forte."

"Give it your best shot, and tell me why you consider this victory a betrayal. Mark knew you planned to win."

Leanne snorted. "But he didn't imagine I could, and I don't think he thought I'd go through with it."

"Why ever not?"

Leanne glanced over, relieved her mom had to attend to the extra Italian sauce on the stovetop and didn't see her expression. What to tell her and how to phrase it?

Unfortunately, her thoughts took too long. "Leanne, what are you up to? Oh, my gosh. You're in love with Mark."

"Not love," she objected. "Infatuated, maybe."

"Hmm-mm."

"I don't know why I came here if you're not going to believe me."

"You came, my darling, because you know I'm on your side. But I'm not blind to your faults."

"What faults?" Leanne said.

Her mother folded her arms across her chest.

"Oh, those," Leanne muttered.

"In particular," her mom said, "your inability to see what's right in front of you."

"A vegetable tray." She tilted it toward the light. "A rather attractive one, if I do say so myself."

"Don't be sassy, and don't try to change the subject." Her mom surprised her by spinning her around and giving her a smothering bear hug.

Leanne laughed. "What's that for?"

"I'm so glad you're in love. Or falling," she amended at Leanne's glare. "Or infatuated."

"I'm not glad. It stinks."

"Yes, it does indeed. So what are you going to do about Mark? Not the contest, but personally?"

"There is no personally. He pretended to want a future with me just to get me to quit CoCo. To abandon the contest."

"That's pretty despicable." Her mom crossed to the table and began to toss the salad. Without turning, she said, "Are you sure he was pretending to care?"

"Of course." But for the first time, Leanne considered the question. She'd *been* sure.

What if she'd been wrong? What if Mark had really wanted to start something?

She put a hand to her forehead, closing her eyes. Had he been sincere in wanting to get to know her, in starting a relationship? Had she turned his innocent suggestion that she quit into a deception he'd never intended? Could she have so misread him?

"Mom, I can't stay." She turned. "I'm sorry."

Her mom opened her mouth, then closed it without objecting. "Whatever you want, honey."

"I couldn't eat, and I'll be lousy company."

Her mom took her hands and held her gaze. "Let me say one thing before you go. Consider which you'd regret losing more, Mark or CoCo."

"I can't have both, but I may not get either one."

MARK DOWNED the whiskey in his glass and slouched against his sofa. Half a bottle hadn't made him feel any better, but at least he felt less.

Damn her, anyway.

Leanne knew what the company meant to him. For her, the challenge was a lark, just to see if she could compete on his level. She had her teaching job as a safety net. Either way, she won.

And what did he have if he lost?

"My good friend, Jack." He poured himself some more whiskey, then planted his feet on the coffee table. Who would censure him? No one. He was alone.

"Alone and at peace," he assured the room, the far side of which had a pleasant, soft appeal. When the whole place turned fuzzy, he'd go to bed. Or pass out here. What the hell did it matter?

He'd offered her... He couldn't remember exactly. His

heart? No, but something. Starting something up, he thought. Getting together. He waved his hand. Whatever.

She hadn't wanted it. Hadn't wanted him.

Then she'd stabbed him in the back to ensure he got the message.

He drained back the liquor. Oh, he'd gotten her message all right. And he'd get back to her about it in the morning. Late morning, he thought, sliding down to rest his head for a moment. Afternoon maybe.

Chapter Nine

Leanne debated the matter, sitting at her temporary desk at Collins the next morning. Her mother's words repeated in her head. Which did she want, Mark or the Collins Company?

If she gave up the challenge and forfeited the stocks and CEO position to Mark, she'd lose CoCo. But did it necessarily follow she'd win Mark?

Had he ever wanted her? Did he still?

She groaned and dropped her head into her hands. A sleepless night with these same thoughts should have been sufficient time to come to a decision. She hadn't. Too much depended on Mark's feelings.

Several times, she'd tried to come up with an answer without considering the impact on him. A strong business leader didn't allow emotion to rule her. Even taking him out of the equation hadn't presented a solution.

Her feelings about giving up CoCo confused her. She thought it wouldn't bother her. Having eschewed anything Collins-related all her life, why would she want the company now? Yet a part of her had enjoyed ferreting out the information regarding Accessories, Inc., for the first task in the challenge. Adrenaline had pulsed through her when she'd approached Art Keller at the restaurant.

Competition flowed through her veins, an evil inheritance from Lionel. *Evil* because without it, she would give up the fight for Collins without a second's hesitation.

Unfortunately, her blood gushed with the need to win.

Damn it all. Why should she have to give up the company and something she'd discovered she loved to do, for a man? Without a guarantee she'd win the man, for that matter. Did he for one moment ever consider giving up Collins for her? Not likely.

A knock interrupted her thoughts. With a gritted smile, she endured yet another Collins executive congratulating her on obtaining the meeting with Kellco.

The door closed, and Leanne let her smile drop. The one person she longed to see darken her door hadn't shown. Back at the university, a grad student was teaching one of her classes today and overseeing the final exam in another just so she could see Mark in person. The ease with which she'd handed over her responsibilities at the school told her where her heart lay.

Part of her wanted to apologize to Mark, and yet another part didn't. She hadn't done anything wrong, just beaten him at his game. So he'd suffered a blow to his ego. He'd just have to be a big boy and get over it.

Grimacing, she couldn't convince herself of this simple perspective. Collins meant everything to him. A job, a reputation, a legacy, but also a family, approval and love.

As much as she wanted the thrill of running Collins, did it mean as much to her?

Of course not. She had a loving mother, a satisfying job,

a solid reputation as both an educator and intermediary between her students and the business world.

A brisk knock sounded on her door, and her heart leapt into her throat. No one but Mark would boldly emphasize his authority by pounding on her door in such a manner. Against her will, her breath quickened and her skin grew warm. She fussed at her hair for a moment, then called for him to come in.

Mrs. Pickett's headful of fluffy white hair edged around the door. Not Mark, but his henchwoman. "Mr. Collins would like a moment at your earliest convenience, Ms. Fairbanks. Come to his office when you can."

"Thank you, Mrs. Pickett," Leanne said. "Tell him I'll be right along."

She held her smile until the door shut. The nerve of the man, summoning her. She glanced at her watch. Eleven-thirty. He planned to squeeze her in just before noon, using a pressing luncheon appointment as an excuse not to spend much time with her. She didn't like his tactics.

It took her five minutes to subdue her annoyance. No good would come of a discussion if she went into it with a belligerent attitude. Moseying down the hallway, she tried to think of calming vistas, gentle music, anything to maintain her composure.

She turned the corner and halted, then darted back a step to peek toward Mark's office door. He stepped out of it preceded by a tall, slender redhead. Julia Simpson from Accessories, Inc.

His hand at her lower back seemed too intimate for a mere business acquaintance. "A comfortable old friend," she thought, then remembered those had been her mother's words. Neither Mark nor Julia made such a claim.

Leanne stood frozen—cold at heart, as well as unmoving. He'd summoned her to come immediately, knowing Julia would be there, and Leanne would see them together. He intended to prove his lack of interest in Leanne.

Mark stepped over to Mrs. Pickett's desk, closer to where Leanne spied from around the corner. He rubbed his forehead. Leanne frowned at the paleness of his face. As impeccably dressed as ever, Mark nevertheless appeared ill. Under other circumstances, she'd guess he suffered from the flu, but knowing of recent events, figured he'd spent a sleepless night, just as she had.

She tried not to care if his inner turmoil had left him awake all night. She hadn't directly caused it. It stemmed from Lionel's will.

Her conscience prodded her. His turmoil *was* her fault. Her victory put him in an untenable position. She knew more than the company rode on Mark's winning.

"Should my expected visitor ever arrive," he said to Mrs. Pickett, his tired tone edged with exasperation, "please tell her I was detained. I'll get back to her when I can."

"Yes, Mr. Collins. Shall I tell her anything else?"

He frowned at Mrs. Pickett. "That will suffice."

Leanne watched them leave, Mark's hand once more resting on Julia's spine. The snake. She heard the disregard in his tone. He'd get back to her? Could he have spelled out his lack of interest in her more clearly?

The heaviness in her chest increased as Mark and Julia disappeared from view. Off to enjoy God knew what afternoon pleasures.

Leanne gathered her things and headed to her office... her real office, she thought, at UIC. A place where she understood the politics, played the games with aplomb, and didn't have tender feelings toward any colleagues. Not a strategic retreat so much as plain old running away.

She could live with that for now.

Once back in her office at the university, though, she couldn't settle. Paperwork called, and she whittled the pile down to manageable proportions for this time of year. She glanced through her textbook for her upcoming summer class, but as she'd taught it before, it held no mysteries for her.

Her languor might be the year-end blues or a late case of spring fever. Summer stretched ahead of her, but she'd have a class to teach rather than a vacation in an exotic city.

Maybe she just needed a break.

She glanced at the walls, the desk, the file cabinets. Familiar sights in a comfortable organizational style. The room embodied her accomplishments at UIC. If she worked in the business field rather than the academic, her office there would look much the same.

It wasn't professional accomplishments she missed. The hole she sensed in her life was love. Husband, children, family.

She wouldn't find her answers here.

SIX HOURS later, Mark rode the elevator to Leanne's apartment on the tenth floor, surprised she'd buzzed him in with so little persuasion on his part. According to Mrs. Pickett, Leanne hadn't come to his office as he'd requested. He thought she'd avoid him at home, too.

Yanking loose his tie, he popped open the top buttons of his white Oxford shirt. A devil of a headache still squeezed his skull, but his stomach had settled sometime that afternoon. Drinking himself into oblivion had been a stopgap. It had felt good at the time, he vaguely remembered, but he needed answers that couldn't be found at the bottom of a bottle.

The elevator stopped, its *ping* piercing his temple. He shoved his tie in his jacket pocket and strode to her door, knocking harder than he'd intended.

She threw open the door, defiance on her face. With her skin flushed pink, breathing labored and eyes full of wildfire, she looked ready to take to bed.

He cleared his throat but couldn't clear his thoughts. She completely captivated his awareness. He'd never last through a discussion with her if he couldn't control his desire.

She'd changed into cutoff jeans and her habitual touristy T-shirt. This one heralded the view from the Hancock Building. Interesting choice, since the Sears Tower stood taller. Supporting the underdog, he thought with approval.

He waited to be asked in, unlike the day they'd gone to Wisconsin. He shut his eyes. He wouldn't think of the disaster that day became. A bad idea turned worse.

"So, why are you here?" Leanne attacked the moment he seated himself on her ridiculous couch. The purplish-red color assaulted his eyeballs and nauseated his stomach. He kept his peripheral vision narrowed away from it.

"To talk," he answered in a reasonable tone.

"I gathered as much. However, I can't conceive of anything you have to say which I would want to hear."

He hid a smile as she reverted to formal mannerisms.

"Mrs. Pickett said you agreed to come to my office today, but you didn't show."

"You were misinformed."

He leaned forward. "She doesn't lie."

"I didn't say she did."

"So you lied."

Leanne sniffed delicately. "As you like."

Mark considered her for a moment. "Well, I'm here now."

"That I can see."

Her condescension started to grate on him. "Because you wouldn't meet with me like a civilized business-woman, I stormed the fortress of your personal abode."

Her eyes flashed but she wouldn't be drawn.

"I want to discuss Kellco," he said.

"More of my research you can capitalize on?"

"What do you mean by that?"

"You took the research I did on the first task," she said, "and pursued Accessories, Inc. Or at least one of its executives."

"Julia? If I remember correctly, after the first task you gave me the information you gathered on Accessories because it no longer had value. To you. I saw the potential for Collins."

Leanne jumped to her feet. "I saw the potential, but I couldn't use it, so I gave it to you."

"Exactly," Mark crowed, rising also. "You gave it to me. Because you aren't in a position of authority at Collins to implement any plan. Then I offered you a place on the ac-quisition team."

"Like Julia would have dealt with me," she scoffed. "I declined in the best interests of CoCo."

"Thanks."

They stared at each other, squaring off like wolves vying to be pack leader.

After a moment, Leanne stepped back, then slid into her chair. He retreated to the couch.

She stared at her hands. "Are you seeing her?"

Her words drifted from her in such a low tone he could barely hear. "Seeing her?"

"Julia."

"No."

Her head raised. Her eyes met his.

"Not in a personal capacity. Just to negotiate the initial terms before our people get together."

Leanne nodded acceptance and dropped her gaze again.

"Why?" he wondered aloud.

"I did come to your office today."

It took him a moment before the pieces connected. He watched her twist her hands together. "Julia dropped in on the chance I was free for lunch."

"And you went."

Blowing me off, she as much as said. He had only one answer. "It's business."

"Right."

"I have an obligation to Collins." He hated speaking to the top of her head. If she'd look at him, she'd read the sincerity in his expression.

Leanne peered into his face and sighed, more disheartened than ever. He meant every word. Business would always come first with him. "Why are you here, Mark?"

"I told you. To discuss Kellco."

She masked her expression, hiding her shattered hopes. She was such a fool.

"I think we should work together on the takeover," he said.

"I won't participate in a hostile takeover of Art's company, Mark."

"But it won't be a hostile takeover now. You've paved the way for Collins. We can buy him out."

"It's not hostile until negotiations don't go your way."

"He'll deal with you," Mark said.

"So why would I need you?"

His expression turned stony. After a minute, he said, "I *am* Collins. If you take the company, you'll have to rebuild it. I'm the continuation of the line."

She offered him a smirk. "Not that heir-apparent crap again? Because, you see, Mark, I'm a direct descendant."

He flinched, and she knew her target had hit. So did the guilt. *Low blow, Fairbanks.*

"We should work together," he said through gritted teeth, "to offer the Collins reputation as part of the sale."

She snorted. "It's Collins's reputation that made Art *not* want to deal with you."

"Collins," he continued, "has never dismantled a company without reason. Unlike some of the other corporations who are no doubt willing to purchase Kellco, we would only enlarge its facilities and manpower. I have no intention of tearing apart Art's endeavors. However, they need updating."

Mark took a paper from his breast pocket and smoothed it across his knee. Leanne leaned forward, interested in spite of herself. He pointed out areas to update, and she noted similarities to her own plan.

We think alike? At the least, they recognized the same deficiencies in a company.

He glanced up at her then. She caught the move and met his gaze. She'd scooted forward until they sat knee-to-knee, heads bent over his rough outline. The light shimmered in highlights and cast shadows in his dark hair. She fought the urge to brush it away from his eyes. Those deep mesmerizing brown eyes.

Her mouth went dry with the need to be nearer to him. She slid back in her chair.

"You don't think these are good ideas?" he asked.

"They're good. I have most of the same notes myself."

"Then what? You don't think we could work together?"

She studied the sunset shining through her blinds. "What about all those things you said in Wisconsin? It was an act to get me to quit so you'd win Collins. I get that. But the fact that it happened makes things awkward. Frankly, it makes me distrust you."

He didn't reply, and she didn't turn to face him. After a moment, she heard him fold his paper. He stood, stepped around her and marched to the door.

"Just forget it," he said. "Forget working together and forget Wisconsin." He slammed the door behind him.

She sat open-mouthed, staring at the space he'd vacated. What did he mean by that? She'd said she couldn't trust him, not that she wouldn't work with him at all. She just wanted to make it clear why she had reservations.

Really? a voice taunted her.

Okay, she admitted to herself. Her pride demanded she call his bluff. Damned if she'd be labeled a fool. So she'd let him know she understood his ploy and would have trouble trusting him if he continued to play such games.

No doubt he'd left in a huff at being seen through.

He hadn't been hurt, she told herself. He couldn't be because he didn't love her.

MARK NODDED to Milo, Gloria's ancient butler, who held open the door to her house. He raked his hair into place, sorry he'd come to dinner this evening. He'd already had a hell of a day. However, he'd refused her invitation the night before, not up to hearing how he'd disgraced the family name with his defeat. He couldn't put off facing Gloria any longer.

"Madam is receiving in the parlor," Milo intoned.

They shared a laughing glance at the ongoing joke between them. Both of them tolerated Gloria's pretentiousness. She didn't mistreat her help, but rather lorded over them.

At least something was still funny in the world. With a sigh, he entered the room.

"Pour me a drink, would you?" she called from the settee.

"Hello, Mother."

"Don't be tedious. I've had a hard day."

Mark poured white wine for Gloria and club soda for himself. It might be a while before he drank alcohol again. The previous evening's binge had been one of only a few times in his life he'd gotten rip-roaring drunk.

"I rather thought you'd opt for something more numbing," Gloria said, "after your defeat."

He closed his eyes. Which defeat? he could have asked, but knew she cared about only one.

"How could you have let that happen, Mark?"

His temper flared. "How could *I* let that happen?"

"That girl bested you."

"So I've heard." He reined in his sarcasm. "Gloria, I run the company, but I inherited quite a legacy."

"One you should strive to uphold."

"Really? Because the legacy I'm talking about is one of double-dealings and back-stabbing."

She jerked upright. "What are you saying?"

"The Lion was known as a ball-buster."

"Mark! I dislike that language."

"Well, I dislike having to deal with the fallout. His reputation earns Collins very little respect and some fear."

"One would think in business that's not a bad thing."

Mark rubbed the back of his neck. "It has its uses."

She smiled with smug satisfaction.

"On the other hand," he continued, "it also makes us a pariah. Companies don't approach us for joint ventures. Most of our recent buyouts have been hostile takeovers. It was the Lion's preferred way of doing business."

"Then if he—" Gloria began.

"It's not the best way." Mark held her gaze. "And it's not my way."

After a moment, she sank back onto the cushion. They sat in silence. He hoped her evaluation of his comments would have her considering his side of things. She saw only the success of the company, the money earned and the fear of the Lion's and Warren's business competitors, which she misread as respect.

A few minutes passed, and Mark wondered what had happened to dinner. He checked his watch. When no one came to announce its being served, he assumed Gloria had put dinner back, wanting to discuss the outcome of the second task.

As though reading his mind, she said, "Do you have a plan to overcome this defeat?"

He nodded, although he didn't have an idea at this moment. He would, and soon. "I'm not conceding the game."

"Glad to hear it." She sipped her wine, studying him over the rim of her glass. "What else has you so down in the mouth?"

He grimaced. He'd hoped his misery didn't show. "Don't worry. Collins is fine otherwise."

Her eyes glinted. "Is it that Fairbanks girl?"

He darted a sharp glance at her. "Why do you ask?"

"Because you're attracted to her. I saw your reaction last month when she went all pale at hearing a few simple home truths. But I also know those kinds of women are trouble. Why, look at her mo—"

"Don't go there, Gloria," Mark said in low menace.

She snapped her mouth closed. "It is her, isn't it?"

He debated for a moment but craved her understanding. He stared into his glass and nodded. "I am attracted to her."

Gloria sighed and reclined against the back of the settee again. "Well, do something about it then."

His head shot up. Had he heard her right? "I didn't think you'd advocate *that*."

"Do something," she repeated, "but not anything stupid. Take her to bed."

His jaw clenched. How like Gloria to miss the point.

"Get her out of your system. Just don't make any

promises or imagine it's forever." She sipped from her glass. "These sexual attractions wear themselves out eventually."

He shook his head at himself. Why had he hoped to get sympathy or understanding here? "You don't have to worry about my making promises, Mother. Leanne won't have anything to do with me."

Her eyes narrowed, not with anger as Leanne's tended to, but in calculation. "That's to the good, of course, if she's sincere. Although, it could be a trick to intrigue you."

"'To the good?'" He snorted. "Thanks, Mom."

She flinched at the title. "Don't be spiteful. You know I dislike that common nickname."

Yes, he knew. After a moment, he let his enjoyment of the petty gesture go. If he put his predicament in terms she could understand, maybe he'd get somewhere. "Here's the thing. I can't get her into bed." Which would only be a part of what he wanted. He sought that beginning they'd discussed in Wisconsin.

"I'd prefer not to discuss this, Mark. Just offer the girl some money and get it done with."

"Won't work."

She paused with her glass partway to her mouth. A Machiavellian light entered her eyes. "Why not?"

"She thinks I lack integrity."

Gloria frowned. "Integrity?"

"You've heard of it, surely? Honesty, trustworthiness."

She glowered. "Of course, I've heard of it."

"Just not used in conjunction with the Collins name." He knocked back his drink, wishing for a moment he could stomach something stronger. The action lost much of its dramatic effect when drinking club soda.

Dramatic or not, Mark felt the result of the action. It set a period to his statement, which was fitting. He determined to end the negative reputation Collins had gained under his grandfather's rule.

Leanne's accusation rang true. Art Keller didn't want to deal with him because he'd patterned himself after the Lion. He'd loved his grandfather, but Mark admitted the man hadn't cared whom he ran roughshod over to achieve his goals.

That practice would stop now. Collins Company's reputation would change. Mark didn't mind losing the label of ball-buster. He preferred to be regarded as honorable.

He could almost hear the Lion spinning in his grave.

"I intend to win her over," he told his mother. "I think I know how to do it."

She stared at him. "What are you going to do?"

"Act upon my conscience." Another word a Collins seldom spoke.

Her mouth dropped.

"Sorry, I can't stay for dinner, after all." He rushed from the room. He might not win Leanne's love, but he'd at least gain her respect.

And his own.

Chapter Ten

"What are you going to do about Mark?" Leanne's mom asked her two days later. Saturday, the best day of the week. No school, no CoCo, no Mark. Just speculation about him.

Leanne shrugged, glancing around the living room she'd grown up in. Oh, to be ten again. Well, not ten, with the teen years ahead of her. Maybe twenty-five. Happily graduated from college, a year into teaching at U of I–Chicago, and the furniture in her apartment all paid off.

She frowned. She'd been dating a nice guy back then. What was his name? Perhaps she should look him up. Mark's image swam into her mind, and try as she might she couldn't impose what's-his-name's over it. She laid her head against the back of the couch and sighed.

"Leanne." Her mom touched her arm.

She opened one eye then closed it again, blocking out the concern on her mother's face. "I don't want to talk about it, Mom. It's useless." She sat up, pulling a leg under herself to curl into the corner. Her mom took a seat facing her on the other end, with her back against the armrest and her chin on her knees.

"Why?" her mom asked.

"He doesn't want me. It was all a game."

"You're sure?" When Leanne opened her mouth, her mother held up a palm, like a traffic cop. "Really sure, Lee. Not impressions or guesses. Did you ask him?"

"Yeah, that wouldn't be at all embarrassing." At her mom's glare, she shook her head. "Sorry, but come on. I told him I knew it had been a ploy. He didn't deny it."

"Oh, Lee."

"Mom, I'm not in the mood to rehash this. I'm certain. Let's just leave it alone."

"Fine." Her expression smoothed out. "So it's over."

"Right. Not that it ever started."

"Where does that leave CoCo?"

Leanne grimaced.

"Be honest with me, honey. Do you want the company?"

"I like some aspects of working there. Researching—"

"I'm not talking about working there, Leanne. Do you want to run the company? Take the reins?"

"I haven't won yet. There's one more task."

Her mom waved her hand in dismissal. "For the sake of argument, let's say you've won. Do you want CoCo?"

Leanne shook her head. "They specialize in hostile takeovers. Sure, the companies they acquire usually benefit. I checked into their record after something Mark said. Collins hardly ever buys a company to destroy it. There's no profit in that."

Her mom nodded. "You'd know best. I have little interest in the corporate world. So, what you're saying is you don't approve of the way Collins conducts its business."

"Right."

"You don't feel you should take control and change that?"

"I…" Leanne frowned. "I should, I guess. It would be the responsible thing to do."

"And the most profitable?"

Leanne shrugged. "Maybe not. What are you getting at?"

"Just that these practices you dislike so much are what's made Collins the force it is. Maybe by eating its competitors and smaller businesses, CoCo has gotten stronger."

Leanne thought of Art's nickname for Mark. Mark the Shark. Now she could see how it fit.

"So," her mom continued, "maybe CoCo serves the business community by absorbing ailing companies. It also keeps them on their toes. Maintain a healthy profit margin or be consumed by Collins."

Leanne stared at her mom's innocent face. "Your lack of interest in the business world hasn't hurt your understanding of it any." She stared into mid-space while reviewing her mother's theory. "Hmmm. A benevolent shark."

"It sounds silly when you say it."

"No, I think you're right on target. I don't believe benevolence ever crossed Lionel's mind. His concentration centered on the bottom line. Profit."

Still, the explanation made sense.

"So," her mom said, "do you want to harness the shark?"

Leanne started, thinking she meant Mark. Realizing she referred to CoCo, Leanne's heart rate settled again. Yeah, she'd love to harness Mark. To get him to do as she wished. To make him want her. The company, though…?

"I don't think so, Mom."

"What are you going to do? Give it to Mark? Just walk away from them both?"

Leanne put her hand over her eyes. The weeks since Lionel's death had destroyed her peace of mind. She'd inherited a fortune, challenged a magnate and fallen in love.

Fallen in love? Oh, jeez. She'd have to get over him.

"Lionel should never have made such a challenge," she told her mom. "Pitting family members against each other. I shouldn't have taken up the gauntlet in the first place. Now I have to admit defeat. I'll never survive otherwise."

"Be sure, Lee. Follow your heart."

Not long afterward, Leanne left, with her mind no more settled and her heart no less troubled. It hurt Jenny to see her in such anguish and know she couldn't fix it.

Jenny considered her advice to be right on target. She tried to live by the same motto. She had followed her heart in staying with Lionel after discovering he was married. It hadn't been easy going against her principles, but she'd experienced immeasurable happiness to offset her guilt.

And she'd had Leanne, a blessing she would have missed out on otherwise. As Leanne grew, Jenny had allowed her heart to guide her in matters of discipline and rewards. She'd spent many hours debating whether to cash Lionel's checks and give Leanne more than they could afford on her salary alone.

Following her heart led her to good things. She hoped the same held true for her daughter.

Now her heart pointed her in a new direction. Art Keller. Without second-guessing herself, she crossed to the phone and dialed his number. "Art, it's Jenny. I know we'd planned to go out tonight, but I need to change those arrangements."

"Jenny," his voice crossed the airwaves to caress her. "Did something come up? Are you ill?"

She smiled at the concern in his tone. "No, I'm fine. I don't feel like a crowd. I'll cook for you."

Silence met her ear. Then, "You don't want to go out?"

"No."

"But you're not canceling on me?"

"No." Her throat closed up, making her words emerge as a whisper. "I want to stay in."

He arrived early. His gentle kiss melted some of her nerves. He wiped his palm on his slacks, the move reassuring her even more. With a flourish, he presented her with a single coral rose hidden behind his back.

"Thank you, Art. It's lovely."

"Do you know flowers have a language? The giving of certain colors and types signify different things."

"I'd heard that, but I don't know what they mean."

"The pink roses I gave you before represented grace, which you exemplify." He cleared his throat. "This coral one stands for desire."

"Oh." Her throat closed on tears. How sweet to tell her of his passion in such a way. Although she hadn't known him long, she'd fallen in love with the man.

"Did you cook?" he asked.

She smiled. Her house smelled faintly of lilac, the scent of the candles burning in her bedroom. She'd hoped to have the upstairs lightly scented by the time he arrived. "You're early," she teased him. "The food is still in the fridge."

He laughed ruefully. "Sorry. We can go out to eat."

"Maybe later." She put her hand in his and led him up the stairs. "I'm not being too forward, am I?"

"Not at all."

"It's just that I couldn't eat right now. To be honest, I couldn't even cook."

They reached her bedroom door. Art's gaze scanned the room. Jenny watched him take in the flickering candles, the flowers, and the closed shades. Maybe it had been too much. They hadn't talked about taking their relationship to the next level. She shouldn't have assumed. Now she'd put him on the spot.

He cupped her face in his hands. "We don't have to rush into anything."

"I want to," she assured him.

He brushed a strand of hair away from her eyes, the back of his fingers trailing along her cheek. "I'm not in any hurry. I'm certainly not going anywhere. You don't need to do this just to keep me interested."

She smiled. "Good to know."

"We can wait."

"Maybe you can," Jenny teased.

He grinned. "Let me rephrase that. I don't want you to think I expect this."

"Art," she said, "if you don't want to, say so. But if you're just thinking of me, it's all right. I'm ready."

"I'm more than ready, Jenny, but I don't take this kind of thing lightly. I haven't slept with anyone since Maria."

He'd been celibate since his wife died? "Sex," she said, "isn't something I do for fun." She laughed at his expression. "I mean, I'm taking this plenty seriously."

"All right then." He gathered her into his arms. They didn't talk for a long time after that. Not in complete sentences, at least.

HER MOTHER'S words stayed with Leanne throughout the weekend. *Follow your heart.* By Monday, she decided to surrender the game to Mark. She needed to regain her equilibrium, get back on course. She'd walk away and erase the Collins Company from her life. If she never saw Mark Collins again, it would be for the best.

She slipped into CoCo with her head down, hoping no one would spot her. Within minutes, she had her few things packed in a box beside her chair. Should anyone come to the door, the box was hidden from view. If she hurried through her resignation letter to the contest panel, she could be out of there without anyone's noticing.

The door burst open, and she jumped.

Gloria stood in the entrance for a moment, then came in and closed the door. "Hope I'm not disturbing you." Her tone said otherwise.

Leanne shuffled some papers on her desk, trying to mask her unease, as Gloria took possession of the chair across from her. What could she possibly want with Leanne?

"This farce has continued long enough," Gloria said. "What will it take to get you to give it up?"

Leanne stared at her.

Gloria's huff expressed irritation. "I don't have the patience to play games. You turned down my first, more than generous offer. I'm prepared to double that amount, although why you think you're worth more, I've yet to discover."

Leanne sat back in her chair, fingers steepled against her lips, and studied the woman before her. Gloria had restrained her dyed platinum hair into a tight chignon. Her turquoise wool suit elegantly showcased her compact frame, the skirt just at her knees. Her matching pumps had probably cost more than Leanne earned in a month at the university. The woman had come dressed for battle, intent on shoving her wealth and status in Leanne's face. Unfortunately for her, Leanne wasn't intimidated.

"What makes you think I'll give up?" Leanne asked. A smirk darted across her mouth. "Especially now."

Gloria's lips tightened at the reminder of Leanne's recent success.

One point for me, Leanne thought.

"You're in over your head," Gloria replied. "It's obvious you have little idea what you're doing."

Leanne cocked her head to the side in mock puzzlement. "And yet I have the edge over your son."

Gloria's face turned red and her mouth pursed.

Two points.

"I don't know how you got to Art Keller, although…" Gloria's eyes raked over her. "I'm sure I can guess. Womanly comforts may blindside a man, but Keller will come to his senses before he signs his life's work over to a neophyte."

Leanne maintained an impassive expression. She'd expected Gloria to attack her. Sticks and stones, Leanne could have told her. Gloria's assumptions missed their mark by a mile.

"Is that all?" Leanne said. "Because I have things to accomplish today."

"Other men to ensnare?"

Leanne smiled to hide the sting of Gloria's barb. She'd certainly failed to ensnare Mark. "Not my forte."

"Really? I'd have thought your mother would have armed you with all kinds of tricks."

Leanne straightened, unable to keep from rising to the bait. "Leave my mother out of this."

"But how can I? Without your mother, we wouldn't be in this despicable tangle."

"I disagree. Lionel's the one who cheated on his wife. Then he made out this underhanded bequest. I agree with you, though. He was despicable."

"You have no right to speak of him in such a way."

Leanne stared at her. Gloria, defending Lionel?

"So you and the rest of the family didn't care if Lionel slept around? Mark told me my mother wasn't the only affair he had. I'd say that speaks quite loudly of whose door to lay blame at, don't you?"

"He was only a man," Gloria said.

Leanne blinked. Did Gloria really subscribe to such an outdated attitude? Was believing this absurdity the only way she could excuse Lionel?

An awful thought occurred to Leanne, chilling her blood. Warren. If Gloria felt such a strong need to defend Lionel, might it not stem from the same need to defend her husband? She swallowed, hating herself for having to know. "And was Warren 'only a man,' also?"

"No, he was not, although it's hardly your concern."

Leanne berated herself for the relief she felt on Mark's behalf. And on her own account. Maybe Warren, her half-brother, had been the honorable Collins. Still, she couldn't let her feelings show. "Your husband wasn't a man?" she mocked. "I'm so sorry to hear it."

Gloria's faced hardened. "You think you're clever, don't you? You think Mark will fall for you, but he won't."

Leanne flinched and could have slapped herself for letting Gloria see it. "Mark is my opponent, that's all."

"But you hoped he'd be more. You thought you could trick him into the bedroom and out of the boardroom."

"Gloria, women don't need to operate that way now. It's the twenty-first century. You should take a look around."

"Just stay away from him."

Leanne could have told her she had no worries on that score. Mark didn't want her. He only wanted Collins. But she didn't say any of that. Instead, she pursed her lips as though contemplating the other woman's words. "Mark. Hmmm. That's an idea. If I do have any trouble with Art, that is."

"You might be able to fool Art Keller and you might fool the Collins board, but you don't fool Mark. He can see you for what you are. You're just like your mother."

"What I am," Leanne said, rising to her feet in her anger, "is the next CEO of Collins."

"What you are," Gloria countered, "is a conniving tramp. God knows what you did with Art that he feels he has to pay you with Kellco. Are you blackmailing him, too?"

"It's past time you left."

"I haven't written your check yet. Not that I don't appreciate the histrionics." She clicked open her purse.

"Don't bother. I don't want your money."

"You should take what you can get from me, my dear. It's all you'll be offered."

"I don't need to be given anything," Leanne said. "I'm taking Collins. I'm taking the CEO position and—" She paused for effect. "—*my father's* stocks."

Gloria flinched but recovered swiftly. "I don't think so. Oh, you can delude yourself into believing you've won. But Mark will get Kellco. He may have to explain to their board about Art's new interests." Again she raked Leanne with her eyes. "I'm sure they'll understand the need to wrest control from him before he sells the company for a pittance."

"Get out."

Gloria sighed. "It won't be the first time a man has been led by his zipper. Or rather, misled."

Leanne balled her fists on her desk, recognizing the allusion to her mother and Lionel. "Listen to me, Gloria. If you or Mark do anything to malign Art Keller's reputation, I'll see to it Mark regrets it."

"Oh? You have that power?"

"I have that information," Leanne said. "I can inform the Collins board of the influence Mark's zipper has on him."

Gloria went white.

The accusation wasn't true, but Gloria believed it, which made it an effective threat. Why would she believe it though?

Leanne gasped as the memory struck her. Before the first task, Gloria had encouraged Mark to "charm" Leanne in order to convince her not to compete. He'd refused at the time, but obviously later, he'd decided to take her suggestion, resulting in the charade in Wisconsin.

Her heart ached more deeply with the confirmation of his treachery. Tears stung her eyes, but she took a deep breath and willed them away. She wouldn't show such weakness in front of Gloria. Instead she'd show her how little she cared.

"Your advice to Mark," she lied, "worked a little too well. In his attempts to beguile me, he fell under my spell."

"A matter easily remedied by your absence."

Leanne noticed Gloria's rising color. She believed Leanne's lies. Believed Mark might be compromised in the same manner as Art. Snagged by his zipper.

Leanne steeled herself against the revulsion of her actions. If she drove home her point, perhaps Gloria would back off Art. "I can inform Todd Benton, as executor of Lionel's will, of Mark's attempts to deter me from continuing with the competition. While perhaps not unlawful, they may be considered by a court to be unethical. I don't think the business community will welcome him with open arms when he leaves Collins."

"Mark isn't leaving Collins." Gloria's voice emerged as a whisper, so strong was her fury.

"He is," Leanne assured her. "I'm taking over. I'm acquiring Kellco and winning the competition." She walked to the door and opened it.

Gloria didn't get out of the chair.

Leanne paused, wondering if anger had possession of Gloria's legs, impeding movement. With a shrug, Leanne left, unwilling to remain in the room with Gloria.

MARK SMILED as Art's assistant led him into his office.

"Mark." Art rose and shook his hand. "I'm surprised at your persistence."

"You shouldn't be."

"No, well, I expect not." They sat. "As Lionel's protégé, you've learned to hang on to the bone in your teeth."

Mark smiled at the backward compliment as he was supposed to. He needed to convince Art he was more than a copy of the Lion. "He taught me many things, the most important being how to identify a company worth having."

Art inclined his head. "Kellco being such a company."

"Yes." Mark held his gaze.

"We agree on that. However, I won't sell to you. I can't even discuss this with you, as I've made a verbal agreement with another party."

"Leanne."

"She is one who's expressed interest."

Mark smiled at the noncommittal answer. He loved the thrust and parry of negotiations. The subtleties of language, the balance of how much to say and how to phrase it. "She said as much to the panel convened to oversee the competition. You know about the competition Lionel set up in his will, I take it?"

"I've heard rumors."

"I'll bet." Mark would bet he'd heard specifics as well, but Art's answer satisfied him.

"Look, Mark, I admire your tenacity. I'm surprised I do, as it has annoyed me in the past."

Mark jumped on his words. "Let's put the past behind us. I know you had strained dealings with the Lion. But he's not at the helm of Collins anymore."

"Who steers the helm of Collins seems undecided."

"No, it's not."

Art tapped a pen on his desk. "Are you telling me Lionel named you his successor?"

Mark hesitated. "No."

"Are you telling me the Collins board has designated you as their permanent CEO?"

Frustrated, Mark shook his head. "Not yet."

"Then the helm stands temporarily unmanned. Or should I say unattended?" Art smiled.

Mark clenched his teeth.

"So, I stand by my earlier statement," Art said. "I've made a commitment elsewhere. Talking to you would be a violation of that trust, if not of several laws." His smile showed teeth. "The Lion may not have cared, but I know you wouldn't want us involved in something unsavory."

Outfoxed, Mark could only shake his head. "You're right, of course. I intend to run the Collins Company in a totally aboveboard manner."

Art nodded his appreciation of Mark's message.

"Just be aware that Leanne and I are in the same position. Neither of us has been named successor by Lionel or the panel. Her negotiations, which I don't expect to discuss with you," he added when he saw Art about to object, "are contingent upon her being appointed CEO."

"You're saying she doesn't have the authority to make this deal?"

Mark shrugged and left it at that.

Art tapped his pen, looking into midspace. Mark began to feel his trip hadn't been wasted, after all:

"Then you're also saying," Art continued, "that you don't have absolute authority, either."

Mark stiffened.

"Leanne told me the details, Mark," Art said. "She deals honestly. It isn't in her nature to do otherwise."

Meaning it was in his, Mark supposed. The tar with which the business community had painted Lionel would take a determined effort on Mark's part to clean off Collins's reputation. But he intended to see it done. "You seem to have formed strong opinions for someone who's just met her."

Art explained his three-year partnership with Leanne through the university. He outlined the internship program she'd originated, as well as the yearly parties, such as the one Mark had attended.

"And, of course," Art said, "I've gotten to know her better in the past few weeks."

"While she convinced you to deal with her."

"While I've been dating her mother."

Mark froze, but his mind whirled. "Jenny?"

Art nodded. "She's a remarkable woman. They both are."

"Yeah, remarkable."

He found it highly remarkable Leanne had the nerve to accuse him of being untrustworthy, all the while using her mother's relationship with Art to further her own cause.

So much for honor.

Chapter Eleven

Thirty minutes after leaving Kellco, Mark shoved open Leanne's office door at Collins, then slammed it behind him.

Her hand flew to her chest, covering her heart. "You scared the bejesus out of me."

He took a breath, trying to rein in his anger. It wasn't working. He'd stewed, simmered and boiled all the way from Art's office to hers. Now he was cooked, his control thin.

"What do you want, anyway?" She made the mistake of asking him with too much aggression. It lit his fuse.

Mark planted his hands on her desk, gratified to see the way her eyes went wide and how she leaned back from him in her chair. "I came to see what honor looks like."

"What?" Her beautiful face crinkled in puzzlement.

Her beautiful, lying, conniving face. He'd been stupid, but had wised up upon hearing Art's announcement.

"Honor," he said. "You accused me the other night of being untrustworthy, so I figured you must be full of all those good qualities I lack."

"Mark, what are you talking about? What's gotten into you?" The color seeped back into her face.

You've gotten to me, he could have said—back when it had been true, just before Art had explained why he wanted to deal with Leanne. Keeping it in the family, so to speak.

Now he didn't feel anything toward her but fury. And disgust. Certainly not yearning. Or regret.

"I just spoke to Art Keller," he said.

"And?"

Oh, she was good. Such wide-eyed, innocent confusion. He could almost believe her act. "And," he said, "I found out he's dating Jenny."

There. Let her defend herself now.

"And?"

"And?" Mark floundered. He stood upright, disinclined to be close to her. He jammed his hands in the pockets of his suit pants. "And I know why he decided to sell Kellco to you."

Leanne's eyes narrowed as she sat forward. "He decided to *consider* selling to Collins *through* me because you and the Lion were sharks. He thought he'd get a better deal with me."

"I'm sure he did. After all, he's dating your mom."

She stood, and Mark swore to himself he didn't notice the way her pink dress molded her form. Or the way the color highlighted her creamy complexion. Or the way her hair shone as brightly as her angry green eyes.

"I'd tread very carefully if I were you, Mark. You're implying my mother is prostituting herself to further my career." She glared at him. "Is that what you're saying? Having met my mother, you can believe that?"

"Of course not."

Her posture relaxed.

"I would never accuse your mother of such a thing. I respect Jenny. She's above such behavior."

Leanne tilted her head. "And I'm not?"

"Are you? Because it seems to me more than coincidental for him to accept your proposition when he wouldn't deal with Collins at all."

"It is a coincidence he's dating my mom." She shrugged. "You're the one who named him in the first task and made me have to pursue his business."

"Coincidence I'll buy because anything else would discredit your mother. But it didn't prevent you from approaching him, did it? What would you call that?"

"I call it networking," she shot back. "I knew the man from our joint work with the university. So when *you*—" She pointed a finger at his chest in a way indicating she'd love to jab it in if only he'd come closer. "—brought up Kellco, of course, I pursued it. What else should I have done—said I know this man in a different sphere, and therefore shouldn't use that relationship here?" She grunted. "Get real."

Mark disliked having the carpet swept from under him, but the feeling of an impending fall rushed through him. He'd lost control of the conversation. He knew she had acted coldheartedly, but now her actions sounded reasonable. He continued his attack, although less certain of his ground. "You don't think it was low to use Art and Jenny's relationship?"

"I didn't use their relationship. I used my prior acquaintance with Art." She folded her arms over her chest. "Use what you've got. You taught me that."

She was using what she had to great effect. Mark could

barely think as he tried not to stare at her breasts. Oh, why the hell shouldn't he? he wondered. She pushed them out there for him to—

What had she said? "I taught you *what?*"

She glowered. "To use what you've got. Who you know. Who you can con."

"What are you talking about?" At least her confusing accusation distracted his attention from her chest. Mostly.

"Using people. Manipulating their feelings so you get what you want."

Mark looked away. The Collins Company had earned that reputation, but dammit, he intended to turn it into something to be proud of. Despite his disillusionment over Leanne's hypocrisy, he still wanted to change Collins's image. The mission he'd set for himself remained.

"Yeah," Leanne said on a sigh. She rubbed her temple. "That's what I thought. Why don't you just go?"

"I have plans regarding that," he said. "I can't change the past, I know—"

"I don't want you to try."

"What?"

"You can't change what's happened. Just leave it alone."

"I've got to do something."

"Why?" She dropped back into her chair. "I just want to forget about it."

It? Mark realized they were talking about different things, although he didn't know what. "Forget?"

She waved a hand. "Let's just finish the competition, then one of us will get out of here."

"Why do you want to forget?" he asked, hoping her answer would clue him in to the topic.

Her mouth opened, her brow furrowed. "Why would I want to remember? Although maybe I'll go back to that restaurant sometime with my mom. And Art now, too, I guess. The food was scrumptious."

What restaurant? The Chinese place where they'd first had lunch? The Italian place where they'd both approached Art, but hadn't eaten together? Or…

His gut clenched along with his jaw. Lake Geneva. For God's sake, why would she bring up Wisconsin? He knew for sure he'd never go there again. That she could consider a cheerful family outing to the place where she'd smashed his dreams said a lot about her lack of affection for him.

"Fine," he spat out. "Go to Wisconsin. I'll get you the name of the restaurant so Art takes you to the right place."

"What are you so mad about? I was the one being deceived there." She ducked her head, her hair a golden wall between them. "It's over. Just drop it."

Mark needed to see her expression, but his pride wouldn't let him bend down enough to peer into her face. Still, he couldn't stop himself from asking, "You wanted it to be real?"

"It doesn't matter, Mark, because it wasn't." She raised her head, eyes on fire. "It was a joke on me. Ha ha. Very funny. Now go away."

He stared at her, torn. His pride said walk away, but his heart said maybe he still had a chance with her. If she'd misunderstood his intentions…

But how could she have? a voice asked. He'd talked about them being together. The future. How clear could a guy get?

Still, she thought it had been an act. How would things change if she knew what lay in his heart?

Mark studied her, with her chin in the air, daring him. To what? Trick her? She had no faith in his integrity. Why should he bother when she cared so little that she could believe such things about him?

Her expression slid into one of consideration as they stared at each other. She licked her lips, then swallowed.

He almost leapt over the desk to take her into his arms.

"Are you—?" Leanne stopped to clear her throat after her voice emerged as a whisper. "Are you saying you meant what you said in Wisconsin? About a future?"

He debated with his pride for a moment, then slightly inclined his head. A half nod, barely perceptible. Not committing himself too deeply until he heard some reassurance from her.

"Oh," she breathed.

Silence pulsed in the room. Then she stood. Waited.

Mark rounded the desk with slow deliberation, not taking his eyes from hers. He stopped a millimeter from her.

Her turn.

Leanne took a breath and leaned toward him.

Good enough.

He wrapped his arms around her, bringing her against his body, and lifting her from her feet. Her hands landed on his shoulders. A squealing laugh of surprise and, he hoped, delight, opened her mouth for his invasion. He staked his claim, devouring her. Their misunderstanding had lost them so much time.

He felt her fingers sliding through his hair, caressing his ear, tracing his jawline. His skin quivered to life at her touch. Blood rushed to the surface, then downward, leaving him light-headed. Dizzy with happiness, he could have said. Not that he'd admit such a weak-ass thing out loud.

Mark set her down, gentling his kiss as his hands explored her body. His place. Tonight. No, now.

"I'm giving you the day off," he said against her mouth.

"What?" she replied, still soft from his kiss.

"As head of the company, I approve your taking the rest of the day off." He pulled back to smile into her eyes. "You can go home."

"I'm going home?" Her brow furrowed.

He grinned. "Well, I didn't say whose home."

Leanne giggled. "I thought you meant I couldn't work here if we got together. Sorry. I'm going to forget I ever thought you'd said that."

Mark stopped short. "In Wisconsin?" He had said it.

"Yeah." She turned to the desk, opening a drawer. He saw her remove her purse as though in slow motion, then turn back to him. "You said I should quit Collins. Or at least, I thought you had."

"I did."

She went still. "But you didn't mean it."

"I did." He saw her eyes change, saw the shield go up. What else could he say? He had said it and did mean it.

"But," she said slowly. "you've reconsidered."

Mark stepped back and shook his head.

Leanne set her purse on the desktop. "I don't want to misunderstand you again, Mark. Let's get this straight. You want to start dating?"

"Yes." He took another step back, wishing for a drink. Water this time for his dry mouth. His hopes turned to ashes, choking him. He could see the dissolution of his future in her eyes.

"You have some…some feeling for me?"

"Yes." More than *some,* more than *feelings.* But this wasn't the time for declarations.

"However, in order for me to date you, I have to quit the competition?" Her arms crossed over her chest again, a defensive measure he could take no enjoyment in.

"Mixing business and pleasure is always a mistake."

Leanne turned her back on him and leaned a supporting hand against the file cabinet, a relic from his grandfather's time. He regretted putting her in this storage room where old files awaited archiving. When she'd started, he'd been angry and the act had satisfied a petty streak in him, but he also hadn't believed she'd be at Collins long.

Now, looking at her stiff form turned so resolutely away from him, he could barely remember how he'd misjudged her ability. Leanne's background had prepared her for objective thinking about the company, letting her investigate options such as Accessories, Inc., while he'd been fixated on Kellco.

He wanted to stroke her soft blond hair, pull her into his arms and tell her they would find a way to be together. Her back didn't invite such intimacy.

"See what happens," he said, "when we even discuss a future? We can't both be here. We're at each other's throats, and not in the way I'd like."

"You want me to leave," she said quietly.

"Only the company, Leanne. I want us to be together."

She turned to him. He could barely withstand the anguish on her face.

"You're putting the company before us," she said.

He shook his head. "Of course not."

"You are. You want me to withdraw so you can have CoCo."

"I want you to withdraw so we can be together." His patience strained, but he determined to convince her. "You're looking at it all wrong. Almost purposefully twisting my meaning. Are you trying to keep us apart?"

"I'm looking at it wrong? Let me explain my side of it then, so we understand each other." She narrowed her eyes as her temper flared. "I meet this guy a little over a month ago. He's good-looking and can be fun to be with."

Mark almost smiled at her qualification.

"I like him," she went on. "He turns out to be a great kisser."

He did smile then, not only at the compliment, but because her openness encouraged his hopes.

"Unfortunately—"

His breath caught.

"—he's also my opposition."

"That's got nothing to do with us being together."

She held her palm toward him. "I'm not done. Then he says he'd like to ask me out, but I have to give up a fortune in stocks and the running of a prestigious company."

Mark clenched his jaw. It wasn't like that.

"All on the *chance* we develop feelings for each other. He won't even date me, as a matter of fact, unless I do."

"Leanne, you're exaggerating."

"Are you saying you would give up Collins for me?"

He flinched and knew she saw it. What the hell kind of question was that? Collins ran through his blood.

"Not that I'd ask you to," she said, allowing him to breathe again.

"I'm not asking you to, either," he said. How could she give up something that wasn't hers? "I just don't see how we can go after the same thing and not have it hurt our relationship."

"So I withdraw and we start dating. What if we don't get along? Where would that leave me then?"

"Now who's putting the company first?"

She made a disbelieving sound. "What are you talking about? You can't use that on me."

"You won't date me because you'll lose the company. So you're putting the company before me."

Checkmate, he thought as her mouth dropped open.

"That's not the same thing, at all."

He just folded his arms and waited her out.

After a moment, he realized she had nothing to say. Stalemate, he thought, turning toward the door. No winners.

LEANNE STEADIED herself before entering Art's office at Kellco three days later. Her decision was firm, her composure not so much.

"Hi, Art," she said. "Thanks for seeing me."

He shook her hand then gestured her into the seat across from his desk. "It's always a pleasure."

"Maybe not this time." She took a deep breath. "I wanted to let you know. I'm withdrawing from the competition for Collins."

His brow furrowed. "What?"

"I'm forfeiting to Mark." Even saying his name had her

near to crying. She'd thought her tear ducts would have dried up, as many tears as she'd shed.

"I guess I asked the wrong question. Why are you giving up? This is your birthright, your inheritance."

She shook her head. "I don't want it. I thought I did for a while, but the more time I spent at CoCo, the more I realized how much I love teaching."

Art's expression turned skeptical.

"Really," she said. "I missed being around students, helping them through the intricacies of business philosophy and practice. Inspiring them."

"If you say so."

Leanne knew she hadn't convinced him, but she couldn't blame him for his doubt. She'd pursued the CEO position with a vengeance, for all the wrong reasons. To spite Gloria and Mark. To defend her mother. Not because she wanted it.

"It's like this," she said. "You built Kellco, shaped it into your vision. Ten years ago, could you have walked away, left it in another's hands and gone to build someone else's dream? I'm not talking about selling the company. Just about letting it remain as is, but without you."

Art shook his head slowly. "Put like that, no."

"It's the same thing. I'm building something at UI–C. The programs I've started and others I've been involved in really speak to who I am. I don't feel that passion at Collins."

Oh. She really wished she'd phrased that differently, especially when Art smiled. Her face heated.

"You know what I mean," she said. "I don't wake up excited to go to work there." She uttered a sound like a laugh. "And I *really* hate board meetings. I don't respect Collins's business practices. My mom asked if I shouldn't run the place, change those practices, but I just don't care enough."

He nodded. "Okay. So now what?"

"I'm staying at the university." She bowed her head. "I know this kind of leaves you hanging."

"I hadn't agreed to more than a verbal consideration." He waved his hand as though erasing its importance. "Don't worry about that. I'm not holding you to anything."

They sat quietly for a moment. Then Art said, "How are you, Leanne?"

She started, her gaze flying to his face.

"This is about Mark, isn't it?" he asked.

"No."

"No?"

Leanne sank her teeth into her bottom lip to keep the tears from forming. "I suppose my mother's filled you in."

"Actually, she hasn't. I don't need to be told when someone I care for is hurting. Anyone could see the sparks when you were together, and it wasn't just the competition."

She shook her head. "I can't talk about it." Her voice came out choked.

"I wouldn't expect you to." He rubbed his neck and uttered a soft laugh. "I'm feeling my age."

"What do you mean?"

"You're so much younger than I am. I'd like to hold you and rock you on my lap until you're all better."

She giggled. "I'm a little big for that."

"Yes, but still, I'm feeling fatherly."

His eyes held hers. What message did they convey?

"That's okay with me," she said slowly.

"Is it?" His arm dropped to his side. "Because I may have to do something about it soon."

"You're going to rock me?"

He chuckled. "No."

"Good." She smiled. "Then you're going to…?"

"Propose to your mother."

Leanne squealed and jumped up. She rushed into his outstretched arms. They laughed and hugged tightly.

"I guess this is okay with you?" Art said.

"Oh, yeah." She pulled back, the smile wide on her face. "I'm very happy for you both."

"Don't tell your mom. I'm going to wait until the time is right."

"Of course, I won't tell her. It'll kill me, but I won't. I promise."

"I just wanted to give you time to get used to the idea. You didn't grow up with a man around. It might be a little strange at first."

Leanne returned to her seat. "If that's true, we'll adjust. It's not like I live with Mom."

"Right." He blew out a breath. "I'm relieved you don't object. I'd propose anyway, but I wouldn't want your mother torn between us." He laughed derisively. "Assuming a lot, aren't I? If it came to the two of us, I know who she'd choose."

"It isn't going to come to that, Art. Dad." She chuckled at his expression.

"I wouldn't mind your calling me that, honey," he teased back. "Let's just wait till your mom says 'yes.'" He cleared his throat. "She will say 'yes,' won't she?"

Leanne widened her eyes. "How would I know? My mother doesn't discuss your relationship with me."

"Uh-huh. And if she did, you wouldn't tell me."

"Right."

"I respect that. Don't like it much at the moment, but I respect it." He considered her for a moment. "Now that we're practically family, would you like to discuss your problems with me?"

"We're not family till you actually get up the nerve to propose and Mom accepts." She smiled with bravado if not much sincerity. "And I don't have any problems."

"Mark."

The name jammed home, lodging in her stomach. She shrugged, trying not to appear sucker-punched. "He's not a problem. We had something for about a minute, but it didn't work out."

"Uh-huh."

"You know, *Dad*, I'm really going to hate it if you do that for the rest of our lives."

"Do what?"

"That little skeptical 'uh-huh' thing."

"Well, if you'd tell me the truth, I wouldn't have to doubt you."

Leanne stared at him. He wouldn't let her look away. Finally, she gave in, her shoulders dropping as the tension of putting up a front eased. "You're right. I did care for Mark, but I was telling the truth when I said it didn't work out. It's over."

"Is that why you're leaving Collins to him?"

"No. Yes. No." Hearing herself, she gurgled a laugh. No doubt she sounded as near to the edge as she felt. "Let me try again. No, I'm leaving Collins because I don't want to be there. Yes, I'm leaving it to Mark because I care about him. But no, I'm not leaving just because our relationship didn't work. He's not driving me away. I'm just going."

Leanne paced across the room, then turned back. "The minute I got involved with the Collins family, I changed. I weighed everything the two of them said, searching for insults about my mom. I've become a reactionary."

"How's that?"

"I never intended to compete in the first place."

Art started, the news clearly a surprise. "Yet you did."

She nodded. "Exactly. I overheard Mark and Gloria being nasty, and my common sense flew out the window. A few days ago, I'd decided to withdraw. Then Mark…"

She paused. Even after everything he'd done, she couldn't expose Mark's trickery and make him look bad. "Let's just say, I changed my mind."

Art smiled. "Your prerogative, I believe."

"Maybe. Still, I keep getting angry and doing things I don't want to do. There's another example I won't give, but trust me, I'm not thinking things out before I act. That's unlike me. Unlike the way I used to be before Lionel's will. The way I want to be again."

Art nodded. After a moment, he said, "So what do you want me to do about selling to Collins Company?"

Leanne blinked. "Do about it?"

"Should I sell Kellco to them?"

"I can't make that decision for you."

"I can't sell to the enemy. You're going to be family, Lee." He smiled. "At least, I hope so."

Her heart caught as he used her mother's pet name for

her. Having a dad would be excellent. "Mark isn't the enemy. Not mine, anyway. I don't know how you feel about him. But I can't tell you who to sell to."

"So you're abandoning me."

She couldn't tell if he meant to tease her, but her conscience stung. Still, players changed all the time in deals. "I'd say trust your instincts. Don't sell if you don't want to."

"I'm ready to sell. I have plans for the future." He smiled. "A sudden yearning to travel."

She grinned. "And hopefully a companion to go with?"

"That's the idea. But I've put my life into Kellco. I can't just stand by and watch it be reduced to nothing."

"I understand that, but I can't tell you what to do."

"Tell me this, then. Do your instincts tell you to trust Mark? If this were your company, would you sell to him?"

Leanne hesitated for only a moment. "Collins doesn't profit from destruction. Mark has plans to improve Kellco."

"Does he now?"

She nodded. "He does. I never officially worked there, certainly never got paid for my time or my ideas, so I'm not breaking any trust when I tell you this. Mark really wants your company. Lionel wanted it, and Mark sees the acquisition as a declaration of sorts."

"A declaration?"

"That he's in charge. That he succeeded where the Lion failed." She took a breath for courage and hoped what she did would benefit both the men she loved. "Sell to him but put in provisos. Get the deal you want."

Art nodded, considering. After a moment he said, "Sure you don't want to come work for me?"

She shook her head. "No, thanks. Besides, you'll be off gallivanting around the world."

"True." He walked her to the door. "Any place your mom really wants to see?"

"Planning to bribe her into a honeymoon?"

He laughed. "Whatever it takes."

"She'll go anywhere with you, Art." She hugged him. "Just make her happy."

"That's the plan."

ART ARRIVED at Jenny's with a bouquet, a ritual he hoped she enjoyed as much as he did. Not always able to come up with eloquent words to express his feelings, he let the flowers speak for him. Unfortunately, Jenny had no idea of their meaning, so the words had to form, as well. He'd have to get her a book on the language of flowers.

On the other hand, he delighted in the expression that softened her eyes when he spoke of the meaning of his gifts.

The door opened, and he wiped his palm dry on his pants.

"Flowers." She smiled. Her kiss warmed him. "What do these mean?"

His Jenny. She'd caught on to him quickly. "Maybe they're just an offering to your beauty."

"Uh-huh."

He laughed as she imitated him. No wonder Leanne objected to it.

"Well," he said as he tossed his jacket on a chair, "I wanted red tulips, but they're out of season. I'll give you some of those next spring."

He eyed her, hoping she'd catch the significance of his long-term planning. The corners of her lips lifted as she ducked her head, hiding a shy smile and assuring him his remark hadn't gone unnoticed.

"What do red tulips stand for?" she asked.

"You'll have to wait and see. Of course, maybe I'll give you blue hyacinths instead."

She wagged a finger at him. "You're making me crazy."

He sat on the couch and pulled her down next to him. "This is heliotrope, which isn't as pretty after it's cut. I found a nursery that had forced these to bloom. It's a summer flower in nature."

"I like the purpley-pink shade and the scent." She sniffed the buds. "Vanilla. Does it mean anything?"

Art swallowed, then met her gaze. His heart hammered as he traced a finger along her cheek. "Devotion."

"Oh."

His finger swept across her lips. "Faithfulness."

Jenny closed her eyes.

Was that a good sign? When they opened, shining with love, he breathed again. "Leanne came to see me today."

Jenny blinked at the subject change. "That's nice."

"We talked about selling Kellco."

She waited.

"She's leaving Collins, did she tell you?"

Jenny nodded and leaned back against the couch with a sigh. "I told her to follow her heart. She said she was, but I'm not so sure. I thought she was in love with Mark."

"I think she is, too."

Jenny sat up. "Did she say something to you?"

"No, but having recently fallen in love myself, I recognized the signs."

Her eyes widened. "You do? You have?"

"You know I love you. I've told you."

"After we were…upstairs."

"I've said it when we weren't making love."

Jenny's breath trembled out. "Since we'd started having sex, I thought maybe you felt you had to say it."

He glared at her. "I love you. Sex or no sex."

"No sex?" She smiled.

"You know what I mean."

"Yes, I do." She reached up and kissed him. "It's happened so fast. I thought it had only happened to me."

"It's true. We haven't known each other long, but I knew I loved you before I said it."

"Me, too. That's why I took you to bed."

He laughed. "I thought I was moving too fast. I didn't want to scare you off. I can't tell you how relieved I was when you made the first move toward the bedroom."

"I vaguely recall your enthusiasm, but you might want to refresh my memory."

"You bet."

She tried to rise, tugging on his hand, but he pulled her back to the couch. "First," he said, "I want to ask you about selling Kellco to the Collins Company."

"Why would you ask me?"

"Because this concerns you." Art took a deep breath. "These flowers represent my feelings for you."

"Devotion and faithfulness."

He nodded. "And love. Jenny, I want to sell the company now because of you. Before we met, I wanted to get rid of it because I no longer cared. I didn't 'wake up all excited about going to work,' as Leanne put it. Now I want to free up my time to spend it with you."

He enfolded her in his arms and kissed her. "I want to be with you. Travel places together. Marry you."

He waited, watched her eyes fill with tears. Were tears a good sign? His heart pounded, and his mouth went dry. Had he rushed her? "Well?"

"Yes." She threw her arms around his neck and hugged him close. "Oh, yes."

Beyond words and without flowers, her kiss spoke for her.

Chapter Twelve

Leanne entered the boardroom, relieved to see Mark hadn't arrived yet. Her plan must have worked. When she'd asked Mrs. Pickett to help her, she'd worried whether she could count on the woman as her ally. Leanne's idea had been to delay Mark so she could address the panel alone. Once Mrs. Pickett learned her intention, she guaranteed her assistance. Not only had the elderly secretary agreed to waylay her boss, she'd also contacted the panel members with Leanne's request to move the meeting up fifteen minutes.

"Leanne," Harrison Mulvany said as he entered with Mrs. Metcalf and Mr. Garland. Todd Benton, as executor of Lionel's will, entered behind them. "This is highly irregular."

This whole competition had been highly irregular, but she figured he meant starting without Mark.

"I understand that and appreciate your patience. Were this an ordinary circumstance, with us part of a real board, I would never have asked it of you."

She remained standing as they took their seats. Today, she'd dressed in black, too. The five of them looked like an assemblage of crows.

"But we're not a real board," she continued. "I'm an outsider, and you're a panel set up to oversee provisions of a will. Need I remind anyone here, this whole procedure was based on a television program, which makes us even less official? After today, your existence as such will no longer be needed."

Their gasps alerted her to her blunder. She'd taken refuge in formal language, hoping to shield herself from reality and the accompanying pain, but had garbled her meaning in the process. "You will remain as board members of Collins, of course. However, I am withdrawing from the competition, ending your duty here."

She shut out their murmurs, not caring if they protested or celebrated her leaving. Raising her voice over theirs, she said, "Before the first challenge, Mr. Benton, you informed Mark and I if we chose not to compete, the stocks and CEO position would go to the other person. So my withdrawal means Mark will be awarded those now. Did I understand correctly?"

"You did," Benton said. "I'd urge you to reconsider, Ms. Fairbanks. From what the panel has told me, you're not exactly losing this contest."

She inclined her head. "True, but I no longer want to win it. I have something of a conflict of interest."

Mulvany shook his head. "As a prospective board member under your rule, I'd like to assure you of our loyalty."

"Thank you, Mr. Mulvany." She nodded at the others. "All of you. It isn't a matter of allegiance. I simply have no desire to run the company. I'd prefer to leave before Mark arrives and you appoint him the winner."

She slid a typed sheet toward them. "This is my formal withdrawal. Mr. Benton, if you need anything else signed for the purposes of the will, please let me know. I'd like this over with as soon as possible."

Silence settled over the room as Benton glanced through the letter. With a shrug, he put it in a folder. "It appears to cover all requirements. We have no choice but to accept it."

"Thank you."

"Thank you for what?" Mark asked as he came in the door. He glowered at the group. "I wouldn't have expected this of you, Benton."

"Expected what?" the lawyer asked. The panel members glared at Mark, recognizing his insult if not his meaning.

"Meeting behind my back."

"We've done no such thing."

Mulvany and the other panel members added their objections.

"They simply complimented my work," Leanne said, cutting through the dissension. "I thanked them for their kindness."

Mark glared, then shrugged none too convincingly. His gaze fixed on her. "Fine, then. I apologize if I jumped to conclusions. Since I've been detained with flimsy excuses, I became suspicious."

Leanne kept her expression bland, hoping guilt didn't color her skin.

Mark tossed a file on the desk. He didn't sit. "Leanne went first in the first task. I presented my plan first in the second task. So we're even. However, if she doesn't mind, I'd like to go ahead now."

He glanced her way, and she nodded as she took a chair, unable to escape now. His aggressiveness fascinated her. She saw the accomplished businessman he'd become under Lionel's tutelage. Yet this attitude of triumph was new. His voice held an edge, and his gestures filled the room with his presence. Mark dominated now, ruling over the panel members with an authority he hadn't displayed before.

She listened as he outlined his latest efforts with Kellco.

"I persevered and finally persuaded Art Keller to meet with me," he said.

A smile ghosted over her lips. Good old Art. The panel expressed their amazement.

"Hard work," Mark said, not at all humbly. "I convinced him to look at my plan. After that, he could see dealing with me and my team would be in the best interests of his company."

It sounded as though Art hadn't informed Mark of her secret plan to withdraw. Leanne made a mental note to give him a huge hug and kiss.

Mark never looked in her direction as he filled in the panel on his further success. She sat quietly, although each insistent heartbeat sounded louder in her ears. This might be the last time she ever saw Mark. She willed herself not to cry, not to feel the emptiness already building inside her.

"In conclusion," he said, holding up a manila folder, "I offer this agreement, signed by Art Keller, to negotiate with me and only me, as representative of the Collins Company."

He slid the folder to Harrison Mulvany, then seated himself next to Leanne. The panel put their heads together over the page on top. Todd Benton leaned in, as well.

She could feel the heat of Mark's triumph radiating toward her. His success was a bittersweet moment. He'd all but shoved his victory down her throat, yet her pride in him outweighed the betrayal she felt.

Love had sure made her stupid.

Mulvany cleared his throat. Leanne glanced at him and shook her head slightly.

"Well," he said, "it seems Mark has emerged the winner of the contest. We pronounce you the permanent Chief Executive Officer of the Collins Company. Congratulations."

Mrs. Metcalf and Mr. Garland murmured similar words, glancing at Leanne with worried questions on their faces. Mark would be sure to notice soon and inquire into the matter. She couldn't allow that after going to such trouble to ensure he didn't know of her withdrawal.

Leanne stood. "Yes, Mark, congratulations. I don't see any reason for my presence in this room now. I'd like to thank you all for dealing with this in the professional manner you have displayed."

She nodded to everyone, although she avoided making eye contact with Mark, then left. Once in the hall, she breathed a sigh of relief. All her thoughts centered on getting home, to the serenity of her apartment, a warm tub and a vat of ice cream. It sounded like heaven.

Mark watched her go with mixed feelings. He should be popping champagne corks, filling glasses, and toasting his future. He was officially head of Collins. He'd upheld the family name. His father and the Lion would have finally been proud of him.

So why did he want to race after Leanne instead? She'd made her opinion of him more than clear.

Mulvany appeared at his side, prompting Mark to pull himself together. He shook the man's hand. Benton and the others filed out of the room with strange expressions. Puzzled, almost.

Well, Mark was puzzled, too. He rubbed his chest, trying to ease the constriction there. It would be just his luck to suffer a heart attack now. Fate had an ironic sense of humor.

"Pulled it off in the eleventh hour, eh?" Mulvany said.

"Yeah. Threw a Hail Mary." Mark squirmed inwardly. This phony bonhomie was even less his style than sports allusions. Who was he becoming?

"Ms. Fairbanks left rather quickly," Mulvany said.

Mark shrugged. He wouldn't have stayed around to rejoice in her victory if she'd won. Although as he glanced around the almost empty room, he could hardly call this a party. Not even Benton had stayed, and Mark had known the lawyer for more than a decade.

Surely someone would want to celebrate with him?

"I need to tell you something," Mulvany said with obvious reluctance.

A rock sank in Mark's stomach. This couldn't be good. He mentally braced himself and nodded for Mulvany to continue.

"I was trusted with this confidence," the older man said, "but you'll learn of it anyway, and I think you'd want to know now. Start your administration with a clean slate, as it were." Mulvany gestured uselessly. "I don't know how to say it. There's no sense pussyfooting around the issue, so I'll just come out with it." He took a deep breath. "Leanne quit."

Mark stared at him, unable to process the other man's words due to the roaring in his ears. "What?"

Mulvany shrugged. "She gave up. Tendered her resignation. Withdrew from the—"

"I know what *quit* means," Mark cut in, fury starting to build. "What I don't understand is why."

"She said she didn't want to run the company." After getting no response, Mulvany left the room.

Mark stood still, in shock and alone.

Several minutes passed before he pulled himself together. He marched to his grandfather's office. His office now, thanks to Leanne. What had she been thinking? Did she not have enough faith in his ability to best her that she'd just handed the win to him?

He stopped by Mrs. Pickett's desk. The older woman glanced at him, then did a double take. "What's wrong? Didn't you win?"

"Of course I did," Mark growled. Did everyone doubt him?

Her nod and satisfied smile pricked him. "Mrs. Pickett."

"Yes, sir?"

He narrowed his eyes at her. "Did you have anything to do with my winning today?"

"What do you mean?"

"Those delays, for instance."

She waved them away with a careless gesture. "Ms. Fairbanks wanted some time alone with the panel."

"Ms. Fairbanks?" He reined in his temper as she admitted her collusion. "Are you working for her now?"

"No, Mr. Collins," Mrs. Pickett declared, staring him in the eye. "I work for you. I intended to see it stayed that

way. Since that was also Ms. Fairbanks's plan, I cooper-
ated with her. For your own benefit."

Mark planted his hands on her desk, leaning over her.
He squashed the twinge that attacked him at treating a
woman old enough to be his grandmother in this manner.
The battle-ax could hold her own. She proved it when she
tilted her chin at him and raised her eyebrows in inquiry.

"While I appreciate your loyalty," he said, "I'd like to
make it clear that I didn't need, nor do I appreciate, you
going behind my back."

She blinked. "Well, I could hardly do it right in front
of you."

"My point," he emphasized with extreme patience, "is
that I won't tolerate double-dealing. Understand?"

Mrs. Pickett nodded. As he turned away and opened his
office door, she added quietly, "She would have done it
with or without my help."

Mark didn't reply. He entered his grandfather's office,
shivering in its isolated atmosphere. His office now, he
reminded himself again. Maybe if he said it enough, it
would feel right. Funny he'd never noticed the chill, the
space, the emptiness. Probably because he didn't have a
deal to work at the moment. Before, he'd been consumed
with Collins business. No doubt this feeling of being in a
void would go away once he got busy on something.

He sank into the large executive chair and laid his head
back against the leather.

Leanne was gone.

He couldn't get over what she'd done. Why would
she give up? Had she heard of Art's agreement to deal with
him? Maybe Jenny had mentioned something. Had

Leanne thought to save face by withdrawing before he could beat her?

CEO, he thought, looking around at the cavernous space. He nodded. This had been his goal all his life. His destination. His destiny.

He blinked. His destiny was to be alone, running a company? He could picture the entire thing, having seen the Lion live that life since Grandmother had died.

Is that what he wanted for himself?

No, Mark thought. He wanted Collins, yes. But this loneliness would consume him. He'd had a chance at love with Leanne, but mistrust and misunderstandings had ruined it.

He shot upright, heart pounding. Maybe it wasn't ruined forever. What was he if not an expert negotiator? If he could convince a stubborn old enemy to sell him his company, surely he could convince one lovely woman to give their relationship another try.

Jumping up, he raced out of his office, passing Mrs. Pickett without a word. He ignored her soft chuckle, unable to deal with that now. The elevator took forever to reach street level. He practically leaped to the edge of the sidewalk, waving his arm like a maniac. Of all the days not to have his car.

After an eternity on the curbside, he finally got picked up by the slowest taxi driver in the state. Muttering under his breath, Mark cursed the traffic, the signal lights, the driver, and all the guy's relatives. Why couldn't he have been picked up by the usual Chicago cabbie, a driver who zipped between cars and shot through traffic as if he had a death wish? When the taxi pulled over on Rush Street,

Mark bolted out and threw the guy more money than he deserved.

He pressed the buzzer for Leanne's apartment, half amused to find his hands sweaty with nerves.

"Yes?" Leanne's voice came through the box.

"It's Mark. Let me in."

The silence lasted so long, he buzzed again.

"Stop that," she said.

He smiled. That was the feisty woman he'd come to love. Down, but not out.

"Go away."

"You have to let me in." Mark glanced around for inspiration. "I have a paper for you to sign."

"Mail it to me."

"It's from Todd Benton. You have to sign it today to get your money."

"Stuff it."

He laughed, then turned as the sound echoed behind him in a giggle.

A blue-haired lady about three hundred years old stood behind him. A brimless, purple straw hat matched the flowers on her dress. "Trouble with your young lady?"

Mark nodded. "Will you let me in? I need to talk to her in person."

The woman stepped nearer, bringing an overwhelming powdery fragrance along. Mark moved back to give her room to input her code for the door and to avoid choking.

Her pale gnarled finger pressed the buzzer for Leanne's door instead. "Miss?"

"Yes?" Leanne's voice came back.

"Is this man dangerous?" the tiny voice croaked.

Mark rolled his eyes. What would she do if Leanne said yes? Hit him with her umbrella? He eyed her, then slid back just a step.

"Oh, no," Leanne said. "No, he's not."

"You should let him in before I scoop him up," the old lady tittered. "Oh, how cute. He's turning red."

Leanne laughed. "Take him."

"I don't think I'm what he's looking for."

"I'm not, either."

Mark nodded vigorously but put a finger to his lips. He strove to appear virtuous as the woman looked him over, a skeptical moue pursing her lips.

"What's going on, Pauline?" a crackly voice asked.

Mark spun to find another wrinkled face giving him the once-over. This younger woman, only ninety or so, glared at him. "Is he giving you trouble? I have my pepper spray."

"No," Pauline said, as her friend dug in her handbag. "It's a disagreement with his lady friend. He's—"

The door buzzed, cutting her off. Mark darted through. Once outside Leanne's door, he paused to gather courage.

The door opened before he'd found it.

Leanne was still laughing.

"Very funny," Mark said.

She pulled the door wider to let him in. "It made me chuckle."

He rounded on her, causing her to step back. "Why'd you quit?"

She pushed a hand into her hair and sighed. "Oh, Mark. I just did. It's over, okay?"

"No, it's not okay. I want an explanation."

"What does it matter? You won."

He shook his head. "No, I didn't."

Leanne sank onto the couch. "Because I bowed out? You would have won, anyway. You had the agreement with Art."

Mark narrowed his eyes. "Which you set up."

She started. "What are you talking about?"

"You did, didn't you? I'm such an idiot. I can't believe I didn't see it before."

"Don't be ridiculous," she said.

He sat next to her. Would she pull away if he took her hand? "You told Art to deal with me. Then you quit. Why?"

"I didn't want the company anymore," she whispered. "Maybe I lack the killer instinct."

He tried not to wince at her inference. Keeping his voice quiet, he said, "It had nothing to do with me? With us?"

She turned away, but Mark placed his fingers along her jaw and turned her face back to him. He caressed her cheek. "Are you sure you didn't do it for us?"

Leanne shook her head no. Her eyes held onto his.

"No, what? You didn't do it for us?" He leaned in and kissed the corner of her mouth. She remained still, pliant under his touch. "Or you're not sure?"

He touched his lips to the other corner of her mouth. Her almost silent moan raised his hopes. He hovered with his lips just above hers and caught her gaze. "Leanne?"

"Yes?"

"All that stuff I said at Lake Geneva— No, don't pull away." He grasped her hands. "Look at me. The things I said about a future, about dating, seeing where things would lead. None of it was exactly true."

"No kidding?"

He wouldn't let her coldness put him off. "No kidding. I really meant to say, let's skip the dating."

Her gaze darted to his.

"I really meant to say—" He swallowed. "I've fallen for you."

Her eyes went wide. "What?"

"I know, it should be too soon to fall in love. It started in the mausoleum." He laughed uneasily, wishing she'd make a similar declaration and not leave him hanging. "Weird, I know. I've been fighting it."

"You did a good job," she said.

"Not really. I was a goner from the first moment. When I found out about the will, I couldn't believe it. I was furious, partly because I knew it would ruin any chance I had with you."

"Partly?" Leanne smiled.

He grinned sheepishly. "I also felt betrayed. I believed the company was mine."

"And now it is. With or without my decision, you would have won."

Mark nodded. "I'd like to think so. But we'll never know for sure, will we?"

"The competition doesn't matter to me anymore."

"Right," he said. "It's over." He hesitated. "You haven't said anything." *Like, you love me, too.*

She closed her eyes, swallowed. Took a breath.

Mark almost left his skin, the anticipation killing him. Her lids lifted to reveal eyes brimming with tears.

"Your mother won't like us being a couple."

He laughed with relief. "And?"

"And I know what your family means to you. She's all you have left. I don't want to come between you. I'm sure she expects you at her house right now to celebrate."

"I haven't told her yet."

Leanne drew upright. "You haven't?"

"I came straight here."

Her mouth dropped open for a moment. "She'll expect to hear from you immediately. She's probably already gotten the word from her contacts that you've won."

"But I didn't win. At least, I haven't yet." He squeezed her hands, trying to convey his sincerity. "I lost the most important thing in the world to me when you walked out of that boardroom."

"But… Your mother. Being worthy of the family name. All those things you strived for."

"I won't be worthy of anything if you leave me. I'm not looking for anyone's approval but yours."

Her kiss knocked him back against the sofa.

"Are you sure?" she asked, lying atop him.

"I wish I was more sure," he hinted. He held her to him as she tried to pull away. "Of you."

Her frown made him sigh. Why couldn't she just say the words he needed to hear? If he had to ask, he would. "Can I assume from your kiss that we have a chance together?"

Leanne laughed as she understood. "You can assume I'm wild about you."

Mark chuckled. "Took you long enough to say it."

"Then let me be clear. I love you, Mark." She sealed her mouth over his and closed the deal.

Epilogue

Mark pulled into his driveway, glad to be home. His contentment built every night as he drove down his street, no matter what kind of day he'd had at CoCo. Two years before, he and Leanne had purchased an old brick home a drivable distance outside of Chicago. He'd wanted to have a new house built for them, but she'd lobbied for the stately manor she'd found while house-hunting with Jenny. She'd insisted they needed a house in which to entertain his business associates. He'd let her convince him.

She'd been able to reduce her hours in the past year and had recently gone on sabbatical from the university. She consulted for the Collins Company, keeping him "on the straight and narrow," as she liked to tease.

The sound of kids playing in the neighbor's backyard drew him from the garage. Someday his kids would play outside after school, surrounded by friends. He spied the Lexus across the street. Art and Jenny must have arrived before him, back from their three-week trip to France.

Mark opened the front door to discover the older couple cooing over the two-month old infant in Jenny's arms. Little Paul. Mark's chest grew tight just looking at the baby.

Jenny spotted him in the doorway and rose. She crossed the room to kiss him. Mark hugged her and Paul. "You look radiant, Mom. France must agree with you."

"Being married to me agrees with her," Art said, shaking his hand warmly.

Jenny surrendered the baby to Mark, who wasted no time reacquainting himself with his son.

"Paul has grown so much since we've been gone," she said.

"Babies do that, honey," Art teased her. As he'd never had children, his devotion to Paul pleased them all.

Mark's gaze shot around the room while they talked.

"She's in the kitchen," Jenny said with a smile.

He smiled back, sharing the bond of two people who understood the value of love. He went to the kitchen, losing his breath as always at the sight of Leanne, even after four years of marriage. Her smile swelled his heart, and her welcome-home kiss swelled something lower.

"Hi." She cupped his cheek with one hand and the back of the baby's head with the other.

"Hi. What can I do to help?" he asked.

"I'm almost ready, but you can take in the bread."

He set the breadbasket on the maple table, laid out with their fine china and crystal. For Art and Jenny's homecoming, he guessed. How like Leanne to make it an event. He'd have to check if Leanne had gotten some wine from their cellar to celebrate. He inspected the table. No wine glasses, just watergoblets?

Then he did a double take. Five place settings.

Puzzled, Mark carried the baby back into the kitchen. "Why'd you put out five plates? Did Paul graduate to solid food already?" He nuzzled the baby's neck. "You're so advanced for your age." Laughing, he wiped drool off his cheek.

"The extra place is for Gloria," Leanne said.

Mark's mouth dropped. They hadn't seen his mother since she'd boycotted their quiet wedding. Leanne continued trying, enduring Gloria's very vocal disapproval, even after he gave up on his mother. Leanne understood how deeply Gloria's attitude hurt him. She'd sent her mother-in-law pictures of the wedding, their new home and recently of Paul.

He knew Gloria's coming was due to Leanne's efforts. His mother had better keep a civil tongue around Jenny. Although his mother-in-law could defend herself, and she had Art, Leanne and himself to intervene, Mark still didn't want Jenny hurt by Gloria's vindictiveness.

Leanne was trying to blend their families, knowing the night could be a trial. His chest swelled with the realization. Art and Jenny's willingness to endure an evening with Gloria showed their love for him, as well.

"Thank you," he said, kissing Leanne gently.

"Thank me later." She winked at him and sashayed into the living room, glancing back over her shoulder to make sure he watched her. He did.

She joined the couple on the couch. These three people had shared their love with him. Four now, he thought, rubbing Paul's back and feeling the baby's heavy head on his shoulder. Leanne's words from the past returned to him. *You don't earn your way into a family.*

He'd learned that lesson by becoming part of a real family. Leanne's. Maybe his mother would unbend enough to enjoy the same sense of peace and belonging he'd come to know.

"Family," Mark whispered in his son's ear, "is all about love."

* * * * *

as they waited with restless expectancy for her brother.

Michaela squinted, struggling to see through the impenetrable darkness. Everyone looked toward the Elders, but she knew Brody Carter still watched her. Michaela could feel the power of his gaze. Its heat. Its strength. And something that felt strangely like anger, though he had no reason to have any emotion toward her. Strangers from different worlds, brought together beneath the heavy silver moon on a night made for hell itself. That was their only connection.

The second she finished that thought, she knew it was a lie. But she couldn't deal with it now. Not tonight. Not when her whole world balanced on the edge of destruction.

Willing her backbone to keep her upright, Michaela Doucet focused on the towering blaze of a roaring bonfire that rose from the far side of the clearing, its orange flames burning with maniacal zeal against the inky black curtain of the night. Many of the Lycans had already shifted into their preternatural shapes, their fur-covered bodies standing like monstrous shadows at the edges of the forest as they waited with restless expectancy for her brother.

Her nineteen-year-old brother, Max, had been attacked by a rogue werewolf—a Lycan who preyed upon humans for food. Max had been bitten in the attack, which meant he was no longer human, but a breed of creature that existed between the two worlds of man and beast, much like the Bloodrunners themselves.

The Elders parted, and two hulking shapes emerged from the trees. In their wolf forms, the Lycans stood over seven feet tall, their legs bent at an odd angle as they stalked forward. They each held a thick chain that had been wound around their inside wrists, the twin lengths leading back into the shadows. The Lycans had taken no more than a few steps when they jerked on the chains, and her brother appeared.

Bound like an animal.

Biting at her trembling lower lip, she glanced left, then right, surprised to see that others had joined her. Now the Bloodrunners and their family and friends stood as a united force against the Silvercrest pack, which had yet to accept the fact that something sinister was eating away at its foundation—something that would rip down the protective walls that separated their world from the humans'. It occurred to Michaela that loyalties were being announced tonight—a separation made between those who would stand with the Runners in their fight against the rogues and those who blindly supported the pack's refusal to face reality. But all she could focus on was her brother. Max looked so hurt…so terrified.

"Leave him alone," she screamed, her soft-soled, black satin slip-ons struggling for purchase in the damp earth as she rushed toward Max, only to find herself lifted off the ground when a hard, heavily muscled arm clamped around her waist from behind, pulling her clear off her feet. "Damn it, let me down!" she snarled, unable to take her eyes off her brother as the golden-eyed Lycan kicked him.

Mindless with heartache and rage, Michaela clawed at the arm holding her, kicking her heels against whatever part of her captor's legs she could reach. "Stop it," a deep, husky voice grunted in her ear. "You're not helping him by losing it. I give you my word he'll survive the ceremony, but you have to keep it together."

"Nooooo!" she screamed, too hysterical to listen to reason. "You're monsters! All of you! Look what you've done to him! How dare you! *How dare you!*"

The arm tightened with a powerful flex of muscle, cinching her waist. Her breath sucked in on a sharp, wailing gasp.

"Shut up before you get both yourself and your brother killed. I will *not* let that happen. Do you understand me?" her captor growled, shaking her so hard that her teeth clicked together. "Do you understand me, Doucet?"

"Damn it," she cried, stricken as she watched one of the guards grab Max by his hair. Around them Lycans huffed and growled as they watched the spectacle, while others outright howled for the show to begin.

"That's enough!" the voice seethed in her ear. "They'll tear you apart before you even reach him, and I'll be damned if I'm going to stand here and watch you die."

Suddenly, through the haze of fear and agony and outrage in her mind, she finally recognized who'd caught her. *Brody.*

He held her in his arms, her body locked against his

powerful form, her back to the burning heat of his chest. A low, keening sound of anguish tore through her, and her head dropped forward as hoarse sobs of pain ripped from her throat. "Let me go. I have to help him. *Please*," she begged brokenly, knowing only that she needed to get to Max. "Let me go, Brody."

He muttered something against her hair, his breath warm against her scalp, and Michaela could have sworn it was a single word…. But she must have heard wrong. She was too upset. Too furious. Too terrified. She must be out of her mind.

Because it sounded as if he'd quietly snarled the word *never*.

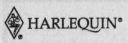

HARLEQUIN®

American ★ Romance®

Three Boys and a Baby

When Ella Garvey's eight-year-old twins and
their best friend, Dillon, discover an abandoned
baby girl, they fear she will be put in jail—
or worse! They decide to take matters into their
own hands and run away. Luckily the outlaws are
found quickly…and Ella finds a second chance
at love—with Dillon's dad, Jackson.

LOOK FOR

Three Boys and a Baby

BY

LAURA MARIE ALTOM

*Available May
wherever you buy books.*

LOVE, HOME & HAPPINESS

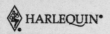
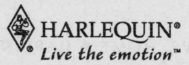

SPECIAL EDITION™

 THE WILDER FAMILY

Healing Hearts in Walnut River

Social worker Isobel Suarez was proud to
work at Walnut River General Hospital, so
when Neil Kane showed up from the attorney
general's office to investigate insurance fraud,
she was up in arms. Until she melted in his
arms, and things got very tricky...

Look for

HER MR. RIGHT?

by

KAREN ROSE SMITH

Available May wherever books are sold.

REQUEST YOUR FREE BOOKS!
2 FREE NOVELS PLUS 2
FREE GIFTS!

Heart, Home & Happiness!

YES! Please send me 2 FREE Harlequin American Romance® novels and my 2 FREE gifts (gifts are worth about $10). After receiving them, if I don't wish to receive any more books, I can return the shipping statement marked "cancel." If I don't cancel, I will receive 4 brand-new novels every month and be billed just $4.24 per book in the U.S. or $4.99 per book in Canada, plus 25¢ shipping and handling per book and applicable taxes, if any*. That's a savings of close to 15% off the cover price! I understand that accepting the 2 free books and gifts places me under no obligation to buy anything. I can always return a shipment and cancel at any time. Even if I never buy another book from Harlequin, the two free books and gifts are mine to keep forever.

154 HDN EEZK 354 HDN EEZV

Name _____ (PLEASE PRINT)

Address _____ Apt. #

City _____ State/Prov. _____ Zip/Postal Code

Signature (if under 18, a parent or guardian must sign)

Mail to the **Harlequin Reader Service:**
IN U.S.A.: P.O. Box 1867, Buffalo, NY 14240-1867
IN CANADA: P.O. Box 609, Fort Erie, Ontario L2A 5X3

Not valid to current subscribers of Harlequin American Romance books.

Want to try two free books from another line?
Call 1-800-873-8635 or visit www.morefreebooks.com.

* Terms and prices subject to change without notice. N.Y. residents add applicable sales tax. Canadian residents will be charged applicable provincial taxes and GST. This offer is limited to one order per household. All orders subject to approval. Credit or debit balances in a customer's account(s) may be offset by any other outstanding balance owed by or to the customer. Please allow 4 to 6 weeks for delivery. Offer available while quantities last.

Your Privacy: Harlequin is committed to protecting your privacy. Our Privacy Policy is available online at www.eHarlequin.com or upon request from the Reader Service. From time to time we make our lists of customers available to reputable third parties who may have a product or service of interest to you. If you would prefer we not share your name and address, please check here. ☐

HAR08

HARLEQUIN *Presents*

Don't forget Harlequin Presents EXTRA
now brings you a powerful new collection
every month featuring four books!

Be sure not to miss any of the titles in
In the Greek Tycoon's Bed,
available May 13:

THE GREEK'S
FORBIDDEN BRIDE
by Cathy Williams

THE GREEK TYCOON'S
UNEXPECTED WIFE
by Annie West

THE GREEK TYCOON'S
VIRGIN MISTRESS
by Chantelle Shaw

THE GIANNAKIS BRIDE
by Catherine Spencer

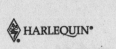
HARLEQUIN®

Mediterranean N I G H T S™

Sail aboard the glamorous Alexandra's Dream
as the Mediterranean Nights series comes to its
exciting conclusion!.

Coming in May 2008...

THE WAY HE MOVES

by
bestselling author
Marcia King-Gamble

As the sole heir to an affluent publishing company,
Serena d'Andrea is very cautious when it comes
to men. But a strange series of mishaps aboard
Alexandra's Dream makes her wonder if someone is
watching—and following—every move she makes.
And when Gilles Anderson constantly seems to be
coming to her rescue, she finds herself watching him.

Wherever books are sold starting the first week of May.

Look for the next exciting new 12-book series,
Thoroughbred Legacy, in June 2008!

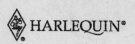

HARLEQUIN®

COMING NEXT MONTH

#1209 THE FAMILY NEXT DOOR by Jacqueline Diamond
Harmony Circle
Josh Lorenz knows he's the last person Diane Bittner wants for a neighbor.
But their preteen daughters have a different opinion. And when the girls start
playing matchmaker for their clashing parents, Josh and Diane have to decide
what really matters. Reliving the mistakes of the past? Or planning their
future—together.

#1210 THE BEST MAN'S BRIDE by Lisa Childs
The Wedding Party
Colleen McCormick didn't expect to fall in love at her sister's wedding...and never
dreams sexy best man Nick Jameson feels the same way! Then the bride bails, and
Colleen and Nick are torn by divided loyalties. With the town of Cloverville up in
arms, the cynical Nick must decide if he trusts in love enough to make Colleen the
best man's bride.

#1211 THREE BOYS AND A BABY by Laura Marie Altom
When Ella Garvey's eight-year-old twins and their best friend Dillon discover
an abandoned baby girl, they fear she will be put in jail—or worse! They take
matters into their own hands and run away with the baby. Luckily the *outlaws*
are found quickly...and Ella finds a second chance at love—with Dillon's dad,
Jackson.

#1212 THE MOMMY BRIDE by Shelley Galloway
Motherhood
An unexpected pregnancy and a thirteen-year-old with an attitude complicate
matters when Claire Grant falls for Dr. Ty Slattery. Claire has had a rocky
past, making her wary of trusting anyone. But can the good doctor convince
her—and her son—that together they can be a family?

www.eHarlequin.com

HARCNM0408